VAIN ART OF THE FUGUE

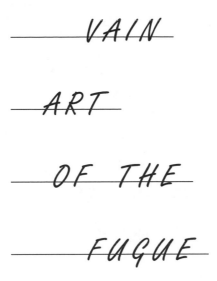

VAIN ART OF THE FUGUE

Dumitru Tsepeneag
Translation by Patrick Camiller

Dalkey Archive Press
Champaign · London

Originally published in Romanian as *Zadarnică e arta fugii*
by Albatros, Bucharest, Romania, 1991.

Copyright © 1991 by Dumitru Tsepeneag
Translation copyright © 2006 by Patrick Camiller

First edition, 2007
All rights reserved

Library of Congress Cataloging-in-Publication Data:

Tsepeneag, Dumitru, 1937-
[Zadarnică e arta fugii. English]
Vain art of the fugue / Dumitru Tsepeneag ; translation by Patrick Camiller.
-- 1st ed.
    p. cm.
"Originally published in Romanian as Zadarnică e arta fugii by Albatros,
Bucharest, Romania, 1991."
ISBN-13: 978-1-56478-421-6 (alk. paper)
ISBN-10: 1-56478-421-5 (alk. paper)
I. Camiller, Patrick. II. Title.
PC840.3.E67Z3313 2007
859'.334--dc22

                                                    2006016854

This publication is partially supported by the National Endowment for
the Arts, a federal agency, the Illinois Arts Council, a state agency, the
Translation and Publication Support Program of the Romanian Cultural
Institute, and the University of Illinois, Urbana-Champaign.

www.dalkeyarchive.com

*Printed on permanent/durable acid-free paper and bound in the United States of America and
distributed throughout North America and Europe.*

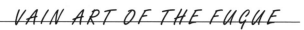

VAIN ART OF THE FUGUE

As I stepped onto the bus I felt an urge to look back, as if someone had called out to me or tapped me on the shoulder or perhaps just looked at me, the way you look at a person who seems familiar and whose name you want to call out (what name?), or the way you stand at the window or the garden gate, gripping the green or black bars, and follow someone with your eyes as long as possible as he walks away, and—for no real reason, knowing he'll turn around anyway—you feel a tightness in your chest as you will him to look back, focusing on the nape of his neck or a point between his shoulders, not thinking of anything, so that people might say you were staring into space down a street that'll soon be empty, where a dog sneaks along the side of the house, and a woman looks vacantly towards the man who's turned the corner, hurriedly walking along with his head slightly bent, clutching a bunch of flowers rather awkwardly, slowing almost to a stop to look at a front yard, unsure of himself, then starting up again, crossing one street and another, approaching the stop where the bus is already about to leave, running the last few yards, jumping onto the step, and glancing back: I couldn't resist the temptation and therefore moved my head with a sense of shame because I couldn't control myself, no one had called out to me, no one was behind me, and then the wheels of the bus began to turn, I climbed the next and final step, felt in my pocket for some change, and the flowers got squashed a little against the ticket-seller's counter.

I SAT QUIETLY FOR A WHILE IN THE SEAT BEHIND THE DRIVER, looking out at the rush-hour streets, but then I began to whisper to him that I was in a great hurry to get to the station and was afraid that I'd miss the train, because, you see, I'm already late and don't feel like rushing from platform to platform (you never know exactly which one to wait on), running around with my coat unbuttoned and tails flapping while people turn and look at me with surprise or indignation; there's no point shouting or waving your bunch of flowers like a flag, faster and faster in that huge, reddish, thick-veined hand, while the train disappears at the end of the platform . . . I'll be left there, head bent and arms dangling at my sides, as I look at my mud-flecked shoes and wonder whether I'm not somehow to blame: that stupid habit of looking for someone to blame, the torture of splitting hairs over and over again. I hear the panting of the locomotive, slower and slower, then the long sigh of relief as it comes to a halt. I turn my head, passengers rush down, the platform fills with people talking loudly and all at once; their words, all more or less the same, collide with one another in the air. Their voices too are very similar, one perhaps thicker or thinner than the next but all strident and rasping, because the noise makes it almost impossible to hear, yet no one can refrain from speaking; the words eventually lose their meaning, or rather they seem to be in a foreign language, and you look around and can't tell what's wrong with you, whether what you see is real or whether you're dreaming.

The driver is wearing a leather jacket and seems very robust. Between us is a kind of glass pane held in place by aluminum bars, and between the glass and the bar on the far right is a space where my voice can get through to him.

"Please go faster, I don't want to miss my train. You see, I took my bags there earlier in a friend's car—he left this morning heading in a different direction. So, I've still got to pick my bags up from the luggage office. I didn't leave this morning because I still had a few things to do: I had to visit someone (there was no point mentioning Maria's name, as he wouldn't have known who I meant, and I'm pretty sure he didn't know Magda either)—anyway, to visit a woman." The driver didn't say a word, as if he were deaf and dumb. At some point a woman with an incredibly large stomach got on the bus; maybe she had a pillow under her dress . . .

It was warm and he felt good. He adjusted the pillow and turned over again, feeling himself begin to fall back asleep. He didn't try to resist, although he knew that in the end he wouldn't be able to stay in bed.

"Get up, you mustn't be late," Maria said, but he kept quiet and turned again to watch her dressing. Then they both went out onto the veranda, where she placed herself right in front of him. With a maternal gesture she adjusted the knot of his tie, smoothed the lapels of his jacket and kissed him on the cheeks. He wanted to kiss her too, but she darted away and descended the few steps to the garden. The gravel crunched beneath her feet. He took the bunch of flowers from the table on the veranda and said, you're right, I should get going. Maria walked with him to the green-painted door: go then, and he left without looking back. A dog with the mouth of a fox stood in his way. In a courtyard a fat man was killing a pig, watched by several women in pink silk dresses, and blood was gushing onto the stone slabs; strangely, the pig made no sound. He didn't stop. He walked on faster and faster, even though he could feel Maria watching him with her fingers still tight on the bars. He didn't look back. He turned the corner onto a street where a cyclist in a top hat and striped jersey was pedalling furiously but not making any progress. A string bag with some fish was behind the cyclist on the saddle rack; he'd probably just been fishing.

Now he saw the stop and broke into a run. He managed to catch the bus right at the last moment.

After giving up one of my tickets, I went to sit behind the driver. "I'm in a real hurry," I said. The driver shrugged: he didn't care. She wired me to wait for her at the station. Do you understand? I've got to be there, on the platform, with this bunch of roses—to meet her as we arranged. The train's never more than ten minutes late, and even if it's later, believe me, I can't risk it. I'll never get the stupid idea out of my head that I'm waiting on the wrong platform, that Magda's train has already arrived on a different one, so—of course—I'll turn on my heels and dash off, first taking long steps and finally actually running back to the front of the platform; I'll have to stop because there are a lot of people at the entrance to the other platform; I'll only just manage to make way for myself. I advance a few yards and again come to a stop. An old man, in thick homemade clothes, seems completely lost in the noisy, excited crowd. He's dragging along a kind of box with a handle. It looks like a soldier's trunk, but he's too old to be coming back from the army; more likely he's been in prison. A tall woman bumps into him as she draws alongside; I look at the woman, and when I turn back he's no longer there. I grip the aluminum bar now until my fist becomes almost white. I lean further forward, to make sure the driver can hear me.

"Maybe you think it's not important: so what if I'm going to meet a woman at the station? But it means a lot to me. Couldn't you go faster, put your foot down a bit?"

The driver's had enough. "Stop bugging me, mister. Get a cab if you're in such a hurry." He was right, although even with a cab I wouldn't have got there in time. At that hour, the streets were really crowded. But he was right all the same.

"It's not your fault," I whispered to him, in a friendly, almost whingy tone. "It's everyone else who's to blame—maybe even myself, although at first it's hard to realize it." Then I shut up and looked out the window. The bus stopped at a red light. Of course the streets were packed, it must have been five or six o'clock, still a long way until evening. Why hadn't I left earlier? Outside, on the pavement, a woman smiled at me: she had Maria's smile, where the lips hardly moved at all, just the corner of the mouth and especially the eyes—dark, shiny, happy eyes. I waved to her with the bunch of flowers and she turned her head away: she was pretending to be indignant, or perhaps she hadn't seen me, hadn't noticed my gesture, hadn't even been looking at me. The bus started up again, and then the woman made a sign to me with her hand. To me? Yes, why not? If I hadn't been in such a hurry, I think I'd have jumped off the bus and gone after her. Or maybe she was waving goodbye, we'll never see each other again, probably that was what she was thinking; she'd wanted to mark our parting in some way. He didn't have a scarf or handkerchief with him, the train was leaving and of course he felt sorry, he'd probably have called out if there hadn't been so many people on the platform—and, in the end, what was the point of calling out? That look is still directed into empty space, soon the street will be deserted, and the woman continues to look vacantly towards the man; he has turned the corner, hurriedly strides along with his head slightly bent, rather awkwardly clutching a bunch of flowers, and very nearly drops them when that dog blocks his path. He recovers his composure with difficulty and takes a few slow steps forward, breathing deeply all the time. Then he crosses the road and turns left onto a street as long and straight as a boulevard, where a cyclist is trying to pedal along—a serious gentleman who looks a little like his father, although his father doesn't wear a jersey, never wore one in his life. Some fish are gleaming in a string bag behind the bike saddle, and on top of them lies a long loaf of bread. The bus was already at the stop, so I ran for it—it's terrible when one pulls away and leaves you standing there. I ran with my coat unbuttoned and tails flapping. People turned their heads and some growled: why's he bothering to run like that, he still won't catch it. And, indeed, that huge, reddish, thick-veined hand started waving faster, and the streetcar will disappear at the end of the platform.

Please step on it, go a bit faster. Maybe I'll still make it in time for the train; maybe it'll be late. I mean, later than usual and later than they've already announced. It may have gotten stuck somewhere in the mountains and is waiting for a snow-clearing team to arrive: the engineer is on edge and doesn't understand why the conductor is so calm or the ticket-collector so talkative—in fact, it's driving him out of his wits. The ticket collector shrugs his shoulders and leaves the engineer's cabin to avoid a quarrel; he's a peaceful man, anyone else wouldn't put up with this engineer. He goes through the compartments, chats with the passengers, assures them it is nothing serious, just a delay of two or three hours, some of which will be made up later. How is it possible? I don't know, madam, I'm puzzled myself: it wasn't such a big snowstorm, and the train ahead of us whistled its way through happily enough. The conductor whistles in turn, causing the bald or shaven-headed man in the corner to jump. He is dressed in a gray cloth jacket and appears to be confused, although he's careful not to gesticulate too much. "I'm puzzled myself," the official repeats.

If the train is so late, it means I'll arrive too early and have to wait in the station like a fool, with those roses in my hand; no, I don't like that idea either. Anyway, it's absurd: who's ever heard of a train being snowed in when it's warm outside, almost summery? No, it's impossible, complete nonsense, not something I can hope for. I'd better try to soften up the driver.

"Couldn't you try to speed it up a little, sir? You see, it's not just a question of my luggage. I mean, that's not really what counts. The luggage, the suitcases, well, I think she sent them on ahead—at least I hope she did. Magda doesn't like having to bother with lots of bags. She's so high-strung."

"Sure, whatever you want," and the man was both amused and touched at the sight of the woman trying to pack all her clothes into one case. She looked very peculiar kneeling on the suitcase to force the lid shut. She was furious.

"Why won't you let me help?"

She wore only a slip and that little pink blouse, leaving her strong, tanned thighs visible. She didn't want help. She was leaving for good: he shouldn't think she'd put up with it anymore, and he said nothing, what was there to say? He stayed silent. His anger had passed, so that in the end, ignoring her protests, he helped her shut the suitcase. Well, it was up to her in the end, but it would still be better to go along with her to the station. Or to go on ahead and buy her ticket. The woman sat down on the edge of the bed, staring at some object in the room. There were not many objects in that hotel room.

The elevator girl made sheep eyes at him, but this time he didn't pay any attention. Once in the street, he began to run: the bus was already there at the stop. Having stepped on board, I cast one brief look behind me—in the direction where the sea should have been but wasn't visible. There was nothing but high-rises and a few trees.

I was annoyed at how slow that man with the thick red scarf was driving. Urging him to go faster made no difference: he paid no attention to my pleas and kept stopping at bus stops and traffic lights. It was as though he did it on purpose.

IT WASN'T TOO FAR TO THE STATION. HE HAD TO WALK DOWN ONE long street, a kind of beltway where most of the traffic consisted of trucks. An occasional cyclist slowly pedaled by the sidewalk, so slowly that you could leisurely examine him: first, in profile, his rough sunburned face, his muscular body beneath a damp and dusty undershirt, his heavy cotton trousers and sandals; then, from behind, the bicycle, which nearly always had a loaf of bread and a few fish in the rack. However slowly he rode, the cyclist still outstripped the walker and eventually left his field of vision—either in the same direction, towards the station, or into a side street on the left or right. The pedestrian was not hurrying. From time to time he stopped, put down the trunk, and wiped his forehead and neck with a large dirty handkerchief. He could feel the sun on his neck, unable to shake off its searing claw except with the help of the handkerchief. The trunk handle had left deep marks in his palm, and he looked at them with amazement—or was it pleasure?—as he drew from his jacket pocket a piece of cloth so dirty and stained that it looked more like a dust rag. Taking a number of deep breaths, he began to rub his neck, then moved up to his bald head—he had a large cranium, with pronounced bumps near the occipital bone—and down over his face. The first sergeant waited opposite him, with a smile that was hard to decipher: a mixture of ironic understanding (perhaps even empathy), indulgence, and disdain, come on, get a move on, what are you waiting for, it was a mocking voice, and then he glanced over at the other two, who were standing at attention and also waiting for the circus to end, for him to get moving again, what the hell, he'd held them up so long and now what was he fiddling around for?—the sergeant was getting quite upset. He put the handkerchief back, picked up the trunk, and set off. He walked slowly and calmly, without hurrying. It wasn't so far to the station, but the trunk felt heavier and heavier, and now the sun's claw had extended its grip to the top of his head. How good it would have been to have something to cover it! At least a baseball cap. Or one of those soldiers' caps. Or even a helmet. Ah, a straw hat with a wide brim, a panama! Although he wouldn't have turned down a felt hat either, even one with stiff sides. A bowler. A top hat. One of the ones people used to wear to the opera.

Another cyclist, this time pedaling faster, and soon turning left down a side street. One step, and another. Left, right, left . . . Now he felt two claws in the middle of his neck; streams of perspiration appeared on his forehead, trickling down into his eyes and past his ears, tickling the curve of his spine. He stopped.

"What are you doing? Keep moving!" The boots of the soldiers in front continued to ring out on the cement. "Why did you stop?" A shout came from somewhere. He turned his head and saw the sergeant red with fury: come on, move, forward march! The other two soldiers stopped and looked back in astonishment. One of them gave out a half-smile, but quickly erased it when he caught sight of the sergeant.

He decided to start moving again: one step, then another, his legs were obedient enough; he wasn't so tired after all, and it would have been stupid to doze off just now. "Come on, speed it up! Left, right, left!" The soldiers' boots clanged rhythmically, and he fell into step with them again.

He walked on the very edge of the pavement. A passing cyclist rode so close that he struck him with his shoulder; he tried to recover his balance by turning the handlebars left and right, so that a fish slipped from the rack and fell onto the asphalt as if into a little river. The cyclist pulled up and began to yell and curse. The walker stopped, put down the trunk and looked at where the tin-plate handle had reddened his palm and fingers. He shrugged his shoulders. He saw the fish slide off towards the middle of the road and then turn left, heading in the direction from which it had come. But the maneuver was unsuccessful: the cyclist saw it out of the corner of his eye and ran off to catch the fish after it had gone about twenty yards; he picked it up, of course, then returned triumphantly to his bicycle and looked around for the pedestrian, who had meanwhile slipped away to the opposite side of the road. For a moment a truck concealed him from view completely, and now there he is hurrying towards the station, best to drop it, no point chasing a guy like that. The cyclist put the fish back in its string bag, on the saddle rack, remounted the bicycle and started to pedal with all his might, balancing his muscular body covered in that sailor's or footballer's vest and heavy cotton trousers, with sandals on his feet and a peaked cap on his head.

There wasn't much further to go. Anyway, there was no need for him to hurry. He fingered the travel permit in his pocket. At the same even pace, though dragging his heels more and more, he continued on down the empty boulevard, at the end of which the station was supposed to be found.

THE BUS STOPPED AGAIN AFTER A HUNDRED YARDS OR SO. THE
driver began to swear, and at first I was afraid because I thought
he was yelling at me. I wasn't the problem, though. He left his
padded, high-backed chair and seemed about to get off the bus,
but then he changed his mind, returned to his seat, and started up
the engine again. The bus lurched forward and covered another
twenty yards or so before a sudden application of the brakes made
me hit my nose against the glass pane that separated me from the
driver. What's got into you? All the standing passengers lost their
balance for a few seconds; one woman fell on her knees, then on
all fours; a little mirror appeared from her open handbag, and a
knife shot out and went under a seat. Two men helped her back
into a vertical position, but almost at once she fell as heavily as
before and two other men rushed forward and lifted her by the
armpits. Having shaken herself free and squatted on her haunch-
es, she ended up almost crawling around the bus in search of the
missing knife, while the other passengers burst into laughter or
made jokes at her expense. Here she is flat on her stomach now,
feeling with one arm under a seat. At last she's found it! She stood

up with the knife in one hand and her handbag in the other. The way she darted her eyes around was almost threatening. The jokes and laughter subsided, and the woman, clad entirely in black, went up to the driver and whispered something, an unfamiliar word or perhaps a name, quite long and complicated, like the name of some medicine, or the flowers in the greenhouses of the Botanical Gardens.

The still leaves of the trees were sketched perfectly on a sky that seemed to have been painted with a single shade of blue. The flowers were mostly roses, also unvarying in their simple brilliant red. Maria put her fork by the side of her plate but kept the knife in her other hand, to drive home the sharp words she was aiming at his face. He continued to eat, looking from time to time through the window into the garden, although he knew that nothing made her angrier. "You should be ashamed of yourself, really ashamed." Her voice was shrill and spiteful, like that of a stepmother reluctant to miss out on any opportunity to scold her unbearable stepson. It was partly the child's fault: he was too pampered and had a room full of toys, especially trains, buses, and other mechanical devices. His adoring father satisfied his every whim, well, it's understandable, but not going quite so far. He smiled and kept his eyes on the plate, then raised them to the breasts bulging beneath her black blouse. He made no reply. "You're just wasting your time. At your age other men have . . ."—and then she stood up from the table and went to the other window, behind him. He turned and caught sight of her face: it seemed calmer than before, no longer the stepmother's, growing more and more beautiful. Only then did he mutter something, something that wasn't an answer—could there be an answer? Still, out of the corner of his eye, he saw that Maria was frowning: not because of what he'd said, but probably because something in the garden had annoyed her. He sat up a little in his chair to look through the window that faced him and saw that the chickens had escaped from the coop. "The chickens," he whispered. The chickens were strutting among the lilies and roses, and he was glad, he was saved, now she would certainly leave and start screaming at Ion, who must be half-drunk and trying to sleep it off; she'd pour out the rest of her venom on him, and when she'd calmed down there wouldn't be time for them to finish their talk. She did indeed leave the room, whereupon he grabbed the knife and fork and began to wolf down everything on his plate. He poured himself another glass of wine, had eaten his fill a few minutes later, and rested against the back of the chair.

He looked distractedly at the old worn furniture in the room: at the tall cupboard filled with dresses that Maria never wore, the threadbare armchairs, the corner chest of drawers that he was not allowed to rummage in, the rocking chair, two or three unexceptional landscapes, and a naively painted picture of a garden (a few trees with leaves carefully outlined against the uniform blue of the sky, and between them some white and red roses). There was also a larger painting, which rather awkwardly depicted Maria with a baby in her arms. The painter had failed to capture Maria's face—not an easy task, it must be said, as her features were highly unstable, and therefore liable to change; besides, she had been much younger at the time, and that was perhaps how she had actually looked.

She was dressed in black, which made her face seem even paler. She held her head slightly inclined to one side. After what had just been going on, this sanctimonious posture was completely unnatural—and, although the other passengers didn't notice it, because her back was turned to them, I was almost entranced by the calm that she managed to impose on herself. Evidently she was an energetic woman, who knew how to make other people listen. The words she whispered to the driver, those long, exotic flower names—or, to be more precise, the Latin terms for them—that she let drip into his ear had the desired effect: the bus now went along smoothly, without a jolt, without even a bump, as if it were gliding on rails; silence reigned inside, no one said a word. I started to have hope again as the bus headed dizzily towards the station; if it keeps on like this there's still a chance, especially since they told me the train is always late, it's not out of the question that I'll arrive just in time. I glanced at the woman next to me, at her pale face and strange look of concentration, maybe she's in a hurry too, maybe she too needs to get somewhere. I noticed how she clutched her handbag to her chest and kept her eyes fixed on the driver's neck or some point between his shoulder blades, and the bus was racing along, barely pausing at its stops; no one protested, now everyone was in a hurry and staring straight ahead.

Maybe the train will be more than ten minutes late, like the woman from Railway Information predicted in that pleasant, slightly husky voice, similar to Magda's.

"Get going or you'll be late," the woman had said, and she looked nice like that, holding the chick in her arms as one would an infant. The chick looked nice too, or anyway funny, with its featherless neck, shriveled red skin, and small bluish crest. Now and then it pecked at the downy white arm that was supporting it. "Look what a beauty she is, my Cuculina!" the woman said fondly, so he had no other choice than to nod a few times in agreement and to stroke the bird himself. He brushed against the woman's warm skin, but she paid no attention and went on looking at the chick. Then, with the other hand, he took her by the waist—or rather, the buttocks—and pulled her down to her knees. The chicken took fright and began to peck hard at the woman's neck and breasts, until finally she let it go.

Magda had plump velvety thighs that he liked to rub against with his cheek. On the table the chicken followed the writhing of their huge torsos with interest. They locked together and drew apart in a rhythm too slow and regular to mean that they were fighting. After a while, the movements of the two large white bodies speeded up to a real frenzy, and their moans turned into stifled yells, or more like a series of grunts. The bird grew scared, jumped from the table and hid beside the chest of drawers, but even there it didn't feel safe. The woman kept up a moaning sound as if she were calling for help, while the chicken opened its little wings as wide as possible and flew towards the blue glare of the window. It managed to climb onto the frame: outside were the garden and flowers, and Ion cutting roses with a large pair of shears. It began to peck at the glass pane, at first timidly, then more and more persistently, but the window didn't shatter and the bird broke off, confounded.

"Look what a beauty she is, my Cuculina!" the woman said, holding the chicken snugly between her breasts. The man lay flat on his stomach in the bedclothes and said nothing. "It's late," she said, and she took the chicken out of the room and began to get dressed: first, the black silk stockings that contrasted so nicely with her skin. The man stroked her hip and thigh: he dug his fingers like claws into her flesh, while she looked away and smiled.

A bunch of flowers lay on the veranda table. "They're for Magda," Maria said. But the man took them and, without a word of thanks, walked quickly towards the garden gate. The woman went after him. She was wearing a long black dress. He turned around when he reached the gate, but she did not let him embrace her; she pushed him away with both hands. "Get going. Don't waste any more time."

He strode along in his unbuttoned overcoat. The bunch of flowers, clumsily wrapped in paper, hung from one of his arms. The street was deserted. In a courtyard, a man with a knife was chasing a pig and two barefooted women in long dresses were holding each other by the waist and laughing. A child with close-cropped hair, sitting cross-legged, was blowing into a flute from which no sound emerged. The walker quickened his pace again and inattentively stumbled into a mongrel that had shot out from behind a side wall. He tottered for a moment but did not fall down. He turned into another street. A couple on bicycles rode out of a passageway: he wearing a striped sailor's or footballer's jersey, she dressed in black. Both were very cheerful.

He broke into a run. The flowers encumbered him, and the tails of his overcoat fluttered like torn wings. A few more cyclists, male and female, overtook him. He saw the bus stop and made an effort to catch it, as it was about to pull away.

HE PUT THE TRUNK IN THE LUGGAGE RACK, NESTLED IN A CORNER, and looked at the peasant with whom he shared the compartment. He too was wearing a rough homespun coat and a pair of boots; he hadn't shaved for several days and his beard was thick and black. Then a man in quite an elegant coat joined them—he had noticed him a little earlier running along the platform, the tails of his overcoat fluttering, a briefcase in one hand and a bunch of flowers in the other; he seemed very agitated and was glancing feverishly all around him; he was probably looking for someone.

Only when the stationmaster gave the signal for departure and the locomotive laboriously screeched into motion did he too decide to climb on board. After putting a foot on the first step, he looked back over his shoulder, as if he had heard someone shout, but no one had shouted to him, and without further hesitation he climbed the steps and moved along the corridor, holding the flowers and briefcase in one hand. He entered a compartment where two other men were sitting, at first sight looking like two peasants, or anyway country people, dressed as they were in thick homespun clothes; one had probably had his head shaved army-style, although he was fairly old and could not have been doing his military service. The two men mumbled something in reply to his greeting: they were obviously not in the mood for conversation, each one dozing in a corner. He went up to the window, opened it, and threw out the flowers, which landed between the sleepers on a parallel track. Then he flung the briefcase into the rack, and noticed there the old soldier's green-painted trunk, a box shaped like a coffin. Didn't the other have any luggage?

Yes, he had a basket stashed away under the seat, between his feet, it was safer there: you never know what might happen on a journey; you doze off and when you wake up it's vanished into thin air. Who can you complain to then? Who can you blame? In the other corner there's an old man who looks like he's just been released from prison, although it's hard to believe he'd start stealing again so soon. And now he's gone to relieve himself and left his box in the rack, surely he can't be up to any mischief. The one with the overcoat is more suspicious: as soon as he came in, he dashed to the window and threw out his bunch of flowers. He must have a screw loose, or maybe it's just an act; now he's calmed down, he's sleeping like a log.

When he returned to the compartment, the old man saw the peasant leaning down and feeling the basket under his seat, and then, not content with that, pulling it out to check that everything was still there: he took out a foul-smelling block of cheese, wrapped in a once-red handkerchief, then reached inside the basket up to his elbows as he carefully replaced it. His large calloused hands reappeared with a transistor radio—it would be better if he turned it on!—but, after looking sadly at the rectangular box that he did not dare hold by the handle for fear of breaking it, he put it back in its place, rummaged around in the bottom of the basket, and came up with a chunk of bread into which he greedily sank his teeth. He chewed slowly and rhythmically with his hairy jaws, and once he'd finished the bread he pushed the basket as far as possible under the seat, then sat thoughtfully with his palms on his knees. The old man was watching him closely.

The door opened and the sergeant came in with two soldiers. He felt his knees tremble beneath the palms of his hands, and when his name was called he stood up and tried to breathe deeply to calm his beating heart. "Hurry up!" the sergeant, or perhaps one of the soldiers, growled. He looked at them a little awkwardly, not knowing what to say, although for several days he had been preparing a speech for this much-awaited moment. He coughed a few times and the sergeant made a sign for him to hurry up; then he realized that anything he said would sound false; he trusted more in looks and gestures, and he would have embraced the other two who had also risen to their feet and were waiting for the awkward moment to pass before lying down again on their beds, but in the end he didn't dare do that either, so he waved to them without much conviction and felt tears welling in his eyes. He looked at one of the soldiers, who was scratching his neck so intensely that his cap had slipped over his forehead. The sergeant shifted from one foot to the other, losing patience. But on his lips he still wore a trace of the smile with which he had arrived; it was hard to say whether the smile expressed indulgence or contempt. "Come on, let's get going!"

He had a gruff voice and was obviously irritated by the awkward movements of the old man, who finally made up his mind to walk towards the door. On the threshold he turned his head, but all he could see was the sergeant's yellowish face; the others were now probably lying back on their beds, still, faces upturned and hands crossed on their stomachs.

Everything then happened very quickly: they were all in a hurry, although they didn't omit any of the necessary formalities or the accompanying gestures they had performed thousands of times before. The station wasn't far away, and although the trunk weighed him down he reached it fairly quickly. The heat forced him to stop from time to time, to wipe his neck, pate, and forehead. There were only delivery trucks on the street, together with a few cyclists, probably workers returning from the market because nearly all of them had string bags filled with bread, meat, and especially fish. One of the cyclists knocked against him, lost his balance, came within an inch of falling, and turned in his seat to curse him. The old man said nothing and crossed to the other side of the road, where there was much less traffic. Certainly no cyclists coming from the station knocked against him. They were all heading towards it.

On the station steps he stopped again to wipe his sweaty brow. Then he went to the ticket office, got his travel permit stamped, and walked unhurriedly to the platform. The train hadn't arrived yet, so he sat on a bench to wait. After a while he saw the young man running as if he were afraid of missing the train; he had a black briefcase in one hand and a bunch of roses in the other. People were looking at him, at first with surprise, then with a kind of indignation when they realized that he was running to the end of the platform and back again, all the time casting anxious looks around him. He's crazy! the old man said to himself, and he lazily stretched his legs. He remained like that, not thinking of anything, gently stroking the rough wood on the trunk with his fingertips.

Eventually the train pulled in. He rose from the bench, vigorously lifted the trunk, and made for a second-class carriage. He lost sight of the young man, who had probably left the platform. He climbed into the carriage and entered a compartment; there was only one other passenger inside—a peasant wearing a grayish-white homespun jacket, with a large willow basket between his feet, half jammed under his seat. He was tired from the journey, his arms and legs ached—he was old, that's all. He sat in a corner opposite the peasant, who watched him glumly and suspiciously through half-closed eyelids. The locomotive whistled, the train was ready to leave, the old man quickly crossed himself, and the peasant, smiling with approval, also made a quick sign of the cross. Then the young man in the unbuttoned overcoat dashed in holding a bunch of roses. The train was already moving when he opened the window and threw out the flowers.

I was still out of breath when I bought the ticket on the bus. The ticket-seller eyed me with ironic sympathy, taking in the flowers and my tousled hair, and broke into a smile.

"I'm in a hurry," I muttered to her. "I'm going to the station."

"Ah, the station," she said.

"Yes, I'm going to meet someone who's been a long way away. He must be an old man by now."

Touched by what I'd said, the ticket-seller put the small plump palm of her hand on mine: it was warm and clammy.

"Come on, cheer up." She stood up from her chair—her breasts were like two melons—and shouted to the driver to hurry up. "The gentleman is in a hurry," she said, winking at me.

The other passengers turned round to look at me. I didn't know what to do, how to behave in such a situation. I bowed to them by way of a greeting. The ticket-seller was very proud of me: she had tears in her eyes. I bowed again, even more deeply. Some people applauded. I raised the bunch of roses as if they were a flag and paraded between the rows of seats. I didn't even look back at the ticket-seller. I felt dizzy with success! I went and sat behind the leather-jacketed driver, who was very broad in the shoulders.

"I think you heard her, no? I'm in a hurry, but you don't seem to care. That's not very nice!"

There was a glass pane between us.

"It's true the train's running a bit late—about twenty minutes, they told me—but I don't want to risk it. I don't know if you understand . . . She'll be upset if she doesn't see me waiting on the platform with a bunch of flowers. She really likes flowers a lot."

"I like flowers too," the woman in the seat next to mine said. Only then did I notice her. She was well built, in the prime of life and with wonderfully white skin: both her hands and her face seemed to be made of plaster. Of course, this impression was particularly pronounced because she was dressed in black from head to foot. On another seat, further down, was a pregnant woman.

I kept trying to persuade the driver. The woman next to me explained that I wasn't allowed to speak to him while he was driving. "So when can I?" I asked, and the woman seemed lost for words. She was a decent woman, probably on her way back from shopping: she had a bag with five fish—tench or perch, I think—and three French loaves. The driver couldn't see my face, and it was very hard to convey to him, with just my tone of voice, the full complexity of the situation in which I had found myself. I turned towards the woman next to me and looked straight in her eyes.

"As you can see, madam, words are getting staler and staler— you can't do much with them at all." The lady smiled with embarrassment. "And the reason is that idiots have used them like so many wheelbarrows, you know what I mean? They've loaded them up with all kinds of idiotic confessions, with all these ideas, each more stupid than the last—and if not stupid, then certainly destructive—in short, with what people call messages."

Naturally enough, the lady buckled under the weight of this argument. She picked up the string bag with the fish and bread that she had placed between our feet—in my excitement I had been accidentally kicking it—and put it on her knees. I stopped talking and drew closer to the window. I looked at the powerful thighs wrapped in the black silk of her dress. Then the accident happened and the driver died. To tell the truth, I'm not too clear about it: I was on the pavement with that black woman in my arms, and I'm sure she liked me, but at that moment she fainted or perhaps died herself, anyway nothing happened to me. I felt puzzled and embarrassed with her in my arms, I didn't dare move for fear of hurting her, I held her tight against me, she smelled good and her body was warm. Bodies don't get cold so quickly! The full weight of her stomach and thighs was resting against me. I put my right arm under her temple and brought my face close to her powdered cheek—up above, in the sky, a long fish was gliding past like a saber.

Suddenly a hand grabbed me by the shoulder and began to shake me. "No, I'm okay, I'm telling you, I'm okay—you'd better check on the lady, make sure she's still alive." A man with a wide drooping moustache was leaning over me. "Why are you being so violent? At least you should have some respect for the dead."

"Are you dead?" the *moustachu* asked, keeping a firm hand on me.

"No," I said, "although, how shall I put it . . ."

He lifted me by the armpits, and once on my feet I no longer knew what to say or what to do—I bolted. They let me go, they weren't that interested in me. I ran scared, bumping into passersby who stopped and swore at me. I remembered the driver: what had happened to him, was he dead? People don't usually survive an accident like that. The steering wheel had smashed into his stomach and crushed his breastbone, or maybe his spinal cord, what a way to go!

I went to find a taxi, as I should have done from the start. Maria, the poor thing, said: "Why keep Magda waiting, you know how excitable she is. And make sure you buy some flowers and take a cab, otherwise you won't get there in time. Come on, cut that out, this isn't the time," and she pushed him away with both arms, "get going!" She smiled, but it was rather a forced smile. He hurried down the stairs, two or sometimes three at a time; the elevator was out of order or he forgot to take it, and anyway—an unimportant detail—not every building has an elevator, or Maria may well have lived somewhere on the outskirts of town, in an old house with a garden; it was summer and before he left the two of them may have sat together at the little table between the flowerbeds, that table with a colored sunshade and butterflies fluttering all around, while Ion's rusty shears cut the red roses that he would tie into a bunch and put on the veranda table. He took the flowers without saying a word, not even a muttered thanks, then went down a few steps on the path, and the gravel crunched beneath their feet. "The flowers are for Maria," Magda said, lowering her head. The man held them as you might a chicken you'd bought at the market. "Come on, get going!"

He went to the window, opened it and breathed in deeply. Then he left without looking back. In the street he broke into a run. The bus was already at the stop.

I was out of breath by the time I reached it. As I stepped onto the bus I felt an urge to look back, as if someone had called out or tapped me on the shoulder or perhaps just looked at me, looked at me for a long time, fixing their eyes on my neck or a point between my shoulder blades: the long look of a woman gripping iron bars, who would like you to look back, just for a moment.

No, absolutely not, you can't have a simple conversation with that guy! Not only is he stupid, he's got pretensions. The ticket-collector left the engineer in mid-sentence and slipped grumbling through the space between the cars. He's unbelievably pigheaded! Or, no, you're just like a big tortoise, that's what he should have said to him, although he's so humorless he might have got angry, sworn at him or even lodged an official complaint about being compared to a tortoise. But he comes in and starts chatting with me, so don't be surprised if one day . . . A train is not a horse and cart, and even when you drive a cart you've got to keep your wits about you. But this big hunk of a locomotive! The poor thing. Who on earth does he think he is, just because he's the driver of an express train now? Let's be serious. Do you think that speed turns you into some kind of royalty, just like that, as though the power of the engine rubbed off on you? Don't you realize how relative it all is, accelerated movement through space? And as for the royalty thing, it's actually the other way round. "What do you mean, the other way round?" "Look, I'll show you: the other way round." And the engineer got furious: "Stop bugging me with your theories! Why don't you just leave me alone?"

No, he wasn't the sort of person you could talk to. A tortoise, an animal with a thick shell, a complete imbecile. All he was ever interested in talking about was women and cycling, nothing else. And he's pigheaded and conceited and uncivil. A complete airhead. If he wasn't so thick he'd have responded in kind, he'd have been able to shut himself up. It wouldn't have been so difficult. If he were in the engineer's place during that conversation about speed, about the connection between speed and beauty, or nobility, he'd have—well, if he'd been sitting there in his place, facing all the buttons and levers on the control panel, he'd have known what to say. He'd have looked over his shoulder and, with a touch of irony, said to the collector: "Excuse me, but you must have noticed that I produce the motion, but that I don't move myself."—"Okay, but doesn't the train move?"—"What's the connection between me and the train?"—"What do you mean? You're the engineer."—"Well, that's precisely the point," and he would have given a hearty laugh. Then, in a cold, mechanical tone: "Listen, are you so sure that this train moves? And if it does move, why is it that we remain in the same place?" Yes, he'd have put an end to his claptrap all right—although, with a bit of an effort, he could have found a reply for the other position too.

The train came into a station where it was scheduled to stop for approximately ten minutes. The ticket-collector stepped down onto the platform. A man ran madly towards the train and stopped when he reached the engine (the engineer had stuck his head out and was looking with an air of stupid satisfaction at the bustle

31

in the station). He was holding a bunch of roses as you might hold a pennant. He looked at the engineer for a second, then turned and again broke into a run—towards another platform, a platform without a train. The ticket-collector looked at his watch. An old man with a sunburned, weather-beaten face was pulling a huge trunk towards one of the second-class carriages. When he went up the steps, you could see that the trunk wasn't all that heavy: maybe it was empty, or maybe the old man was stronger than he seemed. The ticket-collector climbed into the same carriage—the engineer's head was no longer visible—and headed towards the dining car. He felt hungry. He asked for a beer and drank it straight from the bottle. Then he noisily ate the sandwich that one of the waiters had offered as soon as he saw him. With the bottle in one hand and the sandwich in the other, he walked to the kitchen at the other end of the carriage. He spotted something barely moving in a corner: a tortoise that the cook had found crawling around at a station up in the mountains. The cook laughed, showing his tobacco-yellowed teeth. He was a skinny creature, a former sprinter or some other kind of athlete, and the collector liked to chat with him because he knew how to tell jokes, or else funny stories about politics, and wasn't at all stupid.

"How'd you manage to catch it, Pamfile?"

The cook winked at him, drew closer, and whispered in his ear: "It was asleep."

I WAS SITTING BEHIND THE DRIVER, NEXT TO A WOMAN DRESSED in black who had a bag with fish and bread on her lap. I thought I'd seen her before, maybe on a bus or somewhere else; you remember all sorts of faces, even if you've only seen them once. Or was my memory playing tricks? Anyway, it didn't matter: I turned my head and looked out the window. There wasn't much traffic anymore, the bus was racing along, and the woman was smiling rigidly and holding the bars that separated us from the driver.

"It's dangerous," she muttered. I looked at her, surprised. What did she want? Why didn't she just let the driver do his job? He knew the speed limit, and there were enough traffic cops out to whistle, flag him down, and fine him, if necessary.

"I'm in a hurry," I said. "I have to get to the station as soon as possible. I'm lucky the train is supposed to be late—otherwise there's no way I'd get there on time. She asked me to wait at the station, you understand? She wired me, so there's nothing else I can do, and even so the poor woman is pretty worked up; she doesn't know anyone here in town." The woman next to me smiled and held on to the bars. "Please believe me, there's nothing funny about all this. Someone's in a hurry to get to the station, he runs to catch the bus, sits down, and obviously thinks that the bus is going too slowly, that he's got on a snail instead of a bus, and yet we're living in the century of speed, I hope you can agree with me about that, if nothing else." The woman continued to smile. Her face flushed, probably because she felt like laughing and was trying hard to control herself. That annoyed me even more.

"I'm going to the station," I said, raising my voice. "I'm going to meet someone. It's even more important than if I had to catch a train myself. If it were just a question of me, well, I could postpone it, I could leave tomorrow instead. But I'm meeting someone and I've got to be there on time. Understand? It makes no difference whether it's a man or a woman."

To convince herself of this, she had only to look at the flowers, the bunch of roses picked a quarter of an hour earlier from the garden (that is, cut with Ion's shears). Magda had sunk back in the armchair and laughed, her dress sliding up to reveal her tanned thighs.

"You're lying. You said before that you hadn't seen him since he was arrested."

"I've seen him once. In fact, I went to see him a number of times, but they didn't let me in: they told me he'd been taken somewhere else, or that as a punishment his visitation rights had been suspended."

"You don't know if you're coming or going," the woman had said before walking over to the window. She stayed there a long time, her forehead pressed against the glass. Outside, in the garden, Ion was cutting roses. He went and stood beside her, then knelt down and kissed her calves and thighs; she trembled as she felt his lips and tongue move up her legs like warm, sticky snails. She too knelt down, and they made love on the carpet. From time to time the woman moaned gently, then they sighed together and panted as if they'd been fighting.

"Don't forget the flowers," Maria said when it was time for him to leave. She turned her cheek and pulled back her head with an abrupt, decisive movement, all the time holding her hands outstretched, not to push him away but to keep a distance between them. "It's late. You'd better get going." Ion watched the scene unfold, scratching his back with the handle of the shears. His eyes were shining.

He took the bunch of flowers and went off without looking back. He walked along, bent slightly forward, with the flowers hanging just a few inches from the pavement. At one point he slowed down. In a yard, a sturdy man in a vest and a driver's cap had forced a pig onto its back and was about to cut into it with the long knife he was waving in his hand. The pig didn't struggle or squeal: it was waiting for the blow. Three women in silk dresses stood to one side with white bowls as large as washbasins. He stopped to watch the scene. He also noticed a child sitting cross-legged and motionless, in the manner of a Turkish tailor, except that instead of a needle and scissors he was holding a flute. "Hey, Zenon!" one of the women called out, but the child didn't bat an eyelid. The man with the driver's cap plunged the knife into the pig's throat, and blood spurted over his vest. The driver struck a second time. The women hurried forward with the tureens. The pig's blood jetted forth, as if from an artesian well, spattering over the women's dresses. One of them tripped on the animal and fell over it, onto her back. The driver pounced angrily on her, still brandishing the bloodstained knife, while another woman ran off and the third flung aside her bowl and tried to grab the driver's arm. The blood kept spurting from that heap of flesh, soiling their clothes. For a few moments there was silence. Then the man with the flowers heard the child's flute: he was playing a slow melody, full of sweetness; the sky above was clear and he felt happy. The driver stood petrified, his arm still raised. The women and the pig were still; little drops of blood fell from the blade of the knife, in time with the music.

The walker continued jauntily on his way, still listening to the cantilena as it faded behind him. He crossed over and turned left onto a street as long and straight as a boulevard. A cyclist stopped to ask him the time, probably in earnest, although the tone of his voice sounded a little ironic.

"What time does your watch show, sir, if you please?"

He looked at his watch and only then realized how late it was. There was a chance he wouldn't make it in time. He broke into a run. The bus was already at the stop, and he had to sprint in order to catch it.

IT WAS MADNESS TO KEEP LOOKING FOR HER. THE BEACH WAS swarming with bodies sprawled in every position, naked worms in the sand, a tableau that always reminded him of death, or worse, of a rotting corpse or ossuary. The sea was sighing a few yards to his right—a slow, tired panting. Two or three children were playing with a toy bus, determined to push it onto the wet sand. Worms: all were as naked as worms. He took a few steps: a fairly old woman had removed her bra and exposed her large breasts, which drooped down to her waist. A couple of teenagers were holding each other tight and kissing. A child, squealing with pleasure, was pissing into the little waves that broke around his feet.

He gave up. He put on his sandals, not having removed his trousers, and put on his shirt. He climbed the steps to the cliff, stopped at a kiosk and asked for a lemonade. He drank it in one gulp, then asked for another glass. He paid and set off along the cliff: a breeze was blowing and there weren't so many people here. He entered the hotel and asked for his room key, then looked to see whether the Italian's key was in its place and went to wait for the elevator.

The elevator girl smiled at him, as usual. It was only the two of them in there: he could have suggested that she come to his room, although right then, during her working hours, it would be rather difficult. After her shift, then. The girl lived at the hotel, in a room on the top floor. He had asked her which floor it was a few days before, and she had replied immediately, in a warm and natural voice. But right now it wasn't possible. "Still the fifth?" she asked. Was she being sarcastic, or joking? He nodded, but he no longer dared propose a rendezvous. If he had asked her, she would even have told him her room number. But he didn't ask. When the elevator stopped, sure that she would refuse, he asked her if she would like to come and have a cold drink in his room. "It's hot today, very hot." "Yes," the girl said, "but I can't now." "A pity!" he said. "Another time," she said encouragingly. He smiled and left.

He went into his room, lay on the bed, closed his eyes, and tried to fall asleep. After a few minutes, at most a quarter of an hour, he got up and went to the window: the sky was uniformly blue, tiring. He left the room. He didn't call the elevator—he couldn't have taken the girl's half-surprised, half-ironic smile—but took the stairs down. He handed his key in at the reception desk, impatiently pushed the heavy door of the hotel open, and with his body bent slightly forwards, headed towards the cliff. Once there, he stopped and tried to make out what was happening on the beach, as if that were still possible at such a distance. Was she with the Italian? Or had she gone to the nudist camp? He set off for it, but a hundred yards later changed his mind: there was no point, he felt like giving himself a couple of slaps on the face, a buffoon without the willpower to control himself, incapable of waiting a few hours. It was his own fault in the end. Why hadn't he simply accompanied her? He walked aimlessly among the resort hotels and villas. It was hot. He went into an almost empty café, where a sailor was drinking beer alone in a corner. He sat at a table and ordered an iced black coffee. With a lot of ice! The sailor was looking very seriously towards another corner of the room. He put his head on his hands and shut his eyes. He heard the waiter bring the glass with his iced coffee, but didn't move.

He began the old picture game, trying to bring to the surface the oldest, most distant memories, to enlarge them, to give them life (that is, motion), to study each element until it became an image in its own right, as in photo albums in which significant details, often more interesting than the whole, are isolated and made to stand by themselves. This was not at all easy, for he had to ensure all the time that false, imaginary scenes didn't sneak in—dream images or ones he'd fabricated just then out of the elements of real memories; he couldn't always distinguish one from the other, it was very difficult. He saw again the electric train from his childhood, a Christmas present from his father, a truly magnificent train: it used to glide with a melodious tinkling on rails that formed figure eights, slowing down or speeding up in response to one of the colored buttons on the control box. Then came that painful evening! He was sitting cross-legged on the floor, the train was running cheerfully on the rails, and it was a pleasure to watch it and occasionally, like a real stationmaster, to stop it at a platform or a signal—everything depended on you!—and his father was in a good mood and bursting with paternal love as he came into the room, probably wanting to kiss him, and explained a technical detail or a sophisticated railway maneuver, but then trampled on a signal and broke it, he was so fat. The child burst into tears and all but took leave of his senses, starting to punch and kick the man who stood stupidly before him, probably with a terrible feeling of guilt. Apologies and promises had surely followed, but in vain; he banished his father from the room, and the man never again dared to come and play with the train. A few months later he was arrested.

"You're becoming sentimental," Magda said. "In fact, that's what you are: a sappy, sentimental type!" And she rose from the rattan chair and went for a walk on the gravel paths.

"You're lying. You said before that he was arrested much later." Magda had an excellent memory, he saw her bare legs, her dress hitched high above her knees, and she was laughing as she let herself sink back. He took a drink from his glass and looked once more at the sailor, who was himself still looking, captivated, towards the other corner of the café. A man came in with a bunch of flowers and laughingly put them on the bar.

Again he closed his eyes, rested his hands on his temples and tried to pick out only pleasant scenes from his childhood. For a few moments he saw the window with the large golden birdcage that he used to pass on his way to school, the dwarf with the dummy's head— the landlord's dreary joke—and the little dick painted red, the statue in the garden of the old dilapidated house, then, unexpectedly, Maria's face, the golden cage, Maria's face in the golden cage, pale, with ringed eyes, so unbearably sad, and he raised his head and looked despairingly around him.

He paid his bill and walked unsteadily towards the door. Outside, the sun blinded him. He raised his arm as if to protect himself from the claws of a bird of prey, a huge eagle that had swooped down on him. He hurried down the steps to the beach, but the eagle still hovered menacingly over his head; he tore off his clothes, ran into the sea, and swam a few yards at full stretch, then returned to the beach dripping water. He sprawled on the sand and tried not to think of anything. For a few moments he even succeeded. Then the sun settled gently but heavily on his chest, and he felt its eagle claws piercing his flesh. He had to learn to wait, to be patient. He had managed it then, even when it had taken three whole days. It's all about keeping calm and breathing deeply: time passes, you remain crucified in the sand, eyes shut, thinking about nothing—or you think you're thinking about nothing—and you surrender your body to the soft, burning claws of the sun. After a while, you feel Maria's thin fingers on your eyelids, you take her by the wrists and draw her to you, she drops on her knees, you feel her velvety skin, you wrap her in your arms, and now, on the sand beside you, glued to you, it's not Maria but Magda, or neither Maria nor Magda but another, there's some confusion, but what does it matter? it's another girl, the elevator girl or the woman from the refreshment stand and it's so good to rub your cheeks against her stomach and thighs, the bed creaks gently, you can keep your eyes shut, holding just the pillow in your arms, it's all the same in the end.

"It's all the same?" Maria had yelled at him, and she looked both beautiful and absurd standing there in her slip, with her hands on her hips or an arm raised up, threatening. "I'm sick of hearing you play the fool. I'm leaving—I've had enough. Just like I've had enough of your anarchism and all your idiotic ideas. I can't take any more, so I'm leaving."

"Sure, whatever you want, but you've only just arrived." The man watched with amusement the woman's efforts to squeeze all the clothes into one case. They wouldn't all fit: the lid wouldn't shut. "Don't you see you can't manage it?" he said. "Why won't you let me help you?" He liked her thick, suntanned thighs. "Come on, damn it, let me help you." But she didn't want him to. She was going to leave forever. He shouldn't imagine that he could talk her out of it, or that he could dupe her with jokes and last-minute caresses, I know all those tricks. No, no way.

He said nothing: he had nothing to say. The woman sat wearily on the edge of the bed. Her anger seemed to be passing. She looked at him and sighed. "Go to the station and buy the ticket. I want to be alone," she said, almost in tears.

He stood up, went to the window and looked out, his forehead pressed against the glass. In the garden, among the roses, Ion was looking at the sky. Who knows what he'd seen: a sparrow hawk, a star? "Go on—or you'll be late," she said.

WHEN I STEPPED ON THE BUS, I THOUGHT SOMEONE WAS CALLING out to me and turned to look: no one was there. I sat behind the driver, next to a woman dressed in black. I put the flowers on my lap. She was carrying some quite smelly fish in her string bag, with a loaf of bread beside them.

"I'm in a real hurry," I said to the driver, who seemed not to hear me. I said it again, but again it had no effect. I told him I was going to the station and was afraid I'd miss my train. I don't like the idea of running from one platform to another—you never know which one it's going to be—and if I'm late I won't be able to help thinking that I've got the wrong one, and then I'll have to run all over the place, I'll get worked up, and obviously for nothing. It made no sense anyway, because Maria was leaving, not arriving, and now everything was pointless. He ought to go back and ring Magda to ask her forgiveness, to tell her he'd found Maria on the platform with someone else and quarreled with her—a tall guy with a wide-brimmed hat pulled down over his eyes. An Italian or a secret policeman? He went up to them; the man was keeping a peacock on a lead, perhaps he was an animal trainer? Maria pretended not to recognize him and looked away. I must have looked so ridiculous with that bunch of flowers, you know. It was you who urged me to take them, but it was a stupid idea, I shouldn't have gone at all, I should have realized that at some point things become irreversible.

I passed alongside them looking straight ahead, holding the flowers like a candle. I walked to the end of the platform, solemnly, as if I were wearing a top hat. The railwaymen looked at me like I was crazy. One came over and told me to hurry because the train was leaving in a few minutes; everyone had to get on board. Hadn't I heard the voice on the loudspeaker? The voice! I looked at him calmly and said I wasn't interested in such details; I was out for a walk. Then he shrugged and asked whether I had a ticket; if I was caught without one I'd have to pay a fine. I told him I knew that. He looked at the flowers, the engine gave out a warning whistle, I took off my top hat and waved, but only at the engine, not at the slowly moving compartments and the windows filled with heads and furiously animated hands. Then I jumped onto the steps of the last compartment. In fact I'd gotten the platform wrong, but now it was too late. The woman next to me smiled. What did she find so funny in what I'd said to the driver? Perhaps she'd forgotten what had happened a few minutes earlier, when she'd lost her balance and fallen so awkwardly that it had taken four men to lift her back up? What could be going through her head?

The fish began to move in the string bag, opening their mouths to nibble the bread; the poor perch were hungry. The woman hit one with the back of her hand, but then the others thrashed around in protest. Still wearing the smile that she had shone on me a little while earlier, she went on calmly beating the fish. What a fierce woman! Sensing my admiration, fear, or respect— or perhaps all of these mixed together—in the way I looked at her, she turned to me again with that smile, took a knife from her handbag, and cut into a perch's belly. The fish struggled, its mouth wide open, but each movement only hastened its end. Blood soiled the loaf of bread and trickled onto the woman's dress. The fish kept its mouth open, without making a sound, until the moment when it gave up the ghost.

"You're lying," Maria had said, as she scraped off the scales with her knife, sending them flying in every direction; one stuck to her nose, another to her forehead. "You're lying: fish don't have ghosts to give up." He just shrugged and said nothing. She was so beautiful, so clever! She handled the knife with skill and grace, her face shining all the while. He looked out of the corner of his eye at the clock over the white, glass-filled bar; he was afraid of being late but didn't dare hurry her. She herself had to remind him that Magda was arriving that afternoon; she herself had to urge him to go. "You're a big boy now," she used to tell him, "why are you still tied to my apron-strings? Doesn't it bore you?" He protested and kissed her soft white arm; she elbowed him away, not too roughly, but he cried out in pain—a pretence, to be sure. Then came the reconciliation, the kiss on the place that hurt, the long embrace as he watched the hands of the clock; he felt her there nice and warm in his arms: his "darling M."—that was what he used to call her, his pet name for her, just her initial—and she flushed with pleasure. Then she reminded him that it was late and urged him to go; he made her ask again and again, though each time his objections grew weaker. "You can't keep her waiting."—"Yes, you're right, of course." He left without looking back, raced down the five flights of stairs, the elevator as usual being out of order, and tore down the street, his coat open and his tails flapping behind him. People turned to look, some asked indignantly why he was running like that, as if his life depended on it. Maria kept her eyes on him, still clutching the latch on the window. The bus was already at the stop but he still had quite a ways to go; he ran desperately, and even when the big rubber wheels began to turn, one last jump, and I can feel the first step beneath my feet, I grab the handrail, hurriedly climb aboard, feel another step, and still don't turn around, although the woman's gaze pierces my neck like an arrow and I know it'll be stuck there for a long time to come.

Perhaps that's why the woman next to me is smiling. I smile too and gently raise my hand to my neck. She laughs. Then I scratch myself awkwardly and touch the hard sides of the top hat with my fingers. "I'm really in a big hurry," I whisper. "They told me the train's running late, but they don't know by how much. You know, sometimes the engineer manages to make up a bit of time on the way."

THE PEASANT AWOKE WITH A START, LOOKED AROUND, CONFUSED, then leaned down to feel his basket under the seat. The old man was watching him scornfully, but also with a certain sympathy. The young man had vanished; a woman was now occupying his place, and opposite her sat a dark-skinned man with a little moustache, very elegantly dressed, probably a foreigner: Spanish or Italian. The peasant bent down again, pulled the basket a bit forward, ferreted around inside it, and took out something wrapped in several pieces of cloth: no, it couldn't be a child, the woman was watching his movements carefully, there was a large fish inside, a carp or even a barbel, the man opposite smiled at her half-heartedly, almost cringing, then twirled his moustache between two fingers of his hand—or perhaps he was scratching himself. She was irritated by that servile waiter's smile, and at the same time she saw the other man pass in front of her holding a bunch of flowers with comical solemnity, pretending not to notice her as he went up to the tall man next to her and put a hand on the back of his raincoat. Her companion opposite smiled at her but didn't look her in the eye, he was probably contemplating her mouth, chin, or neck; she looked around for the other man but didn't catch sight of him again. Her attention had been drawn to a shaven-headed old man dressed in homespun clothes, sitting patiently on a bench with a dark-green trunk at his feet, like the ones that soldiers have. The palms of his hands had lain on his lap and he had seemed distracted on the platform, not really there, any more than he now seemed to be here in the corner of the compartment, although once and a while he stared at the peasant snoring softly with his mouth open. He sat motionless, and even when the ticket-collector entered the compartment—or later when the peasant woke again with a start and began to mutter incoherently—he barely stirred as he took out his travel permit and handed it over for inspection, without looking up at the official or saying a word.

The ticket-collector looked at him more with pity than suspicion and quickly held out his hand for the other passengers' tickets. The man with the moustache smiled with forced affability, while the woman looked a little sullen, in a short skirt that revealed her thick, suntanned thighs. "Is the train running late?" she asked, and the railwayman replied obsequiously with a long, contorted sentence. The *moustachu*, who clearly didn't understand what was being said, asked something himself, probably in Italian, but the woman didn't answer him and the collector therefore felt encouraged to make his sentences even longer, adding more and more details to his explanation, telling them that an avalanche had brought the train to a stop in the mountains, and contrasting the engineer's impulsive nature with his own much calmer temperament. The Italian gawked as the collector went on chattering and reeling off all kinds of nonsense—about

Pamfile, who had managed to catch a tortoise while it was asleep, and so on, and so forth—while the woman's ticket remained unclipped in his hand. As he spoke, his eyes caressed her suntanned thighs: he paid no attention to the other passengers. She was obliged to thank him several times, bowing her head and holding out her hand for the ticket, and in the end, finally, he didn't dare to continue. He assured her it was nothing serious and handed her back the unclipped ticket, then added one more sentence from the doorway and looked one last time at her legs; now she was explaining everything to the poor Italian, who had been completely overwhelmed by the collector's flood of words. He took a keen interest in all that had happened and shot a glance in the direction of the official, who now was discreetly sliding the door of the compartment shut.

The peasant closed his eyes again. The old man was sitting in the same position and looking at the man opposite—or perhaps he was just looking around vacantly, seeing nothing but the iron-plate door that had just shut on the warder, a scratched and partly rusted door on which everyone gazed with hope and impatience, since one day soon the sergeant would open it and bring the long-awaited news. He sat silently on the edge of the bed, his palms resting calmly on his knees. The other two chatted between themselves, occasionally asking him a question, but he seemed not to hear, or if they insisted, he would answer in a few words without even looking at them: I'm sorry, I'm not feeling well, I don't feel like talking. The others angrily pointed out that he'd been like that ever since they brought him to the cell, or, to be more precise, a few days later, when they released that guy who'd come up with the idea—what an idea!—of an organization to help the communists after they lost power. Isn't that right, Fredi? More or less, but now leave him alone, what can we do if he doesn't feel like talking? And he went on looking at the door: he knew every detail of it, every mark and rust stain, as if he had been studying the map of an unfamiliar region before a trip; this scratch was a forest, that long one trailing across from the lock to the peephole was a river, which flowed into a large patch of rust, a real swamp teeming with poisonous snakes and frogs the size of dogs, their croaks louder than any bark. It must have been terrible at night, like in those dreams of his, with rats and cacti . . . He was naked, running down a hallway decorated with red tulips and filled with rats that swarmed between his feet; he could feel their claws and slobbering mouths whenever he stumbled and fell; he stood up and started running again, trying to escape from a particularly bold rat that was determined to climb his leg like a tree trunk. Then a door opened and a bluish light invaded the hall; he moved towards the opening but lacked the courage to step outside, where the ground was covered with prickly yellow-green cacti snarling upward in the silken glow of dawn. He preferred to remain inside, with the rats, which fell back squeaking into the corners, fearful of the light, or possibly the cacti.

He went to relieve himself in the bucket, then returned to sit on the edge of the bed, his eyes fixed on the door. A few hours later it opened with a loud noise and the long-awaited officer was standing in the cell. Had he come to fetch him? Yes, he had, and he felt he was choking with emotion: he stood up and took a deep breath, to calm the beating of his heart. "Get going!" the sergeant said between his teeth, walking up and down with his hands behind his back. Then he spat into the bucket and ordered a soldier to open the door wide and let in more air. "What are you gawking like that for? Come on, speed it up!" In a daze he put on his boots, looked at the other two men, who were also now on their feet, then at the sergeant, the soldiers standing by the door, and the empty corridor stretching into the distance. He tried to say something, but all that came out were some incoherent sounds; he realized that he had nothing to say and made a gesture with his left hand, bringing it up to his ear and letting it fall again, then buttoned his jacket and walked towards the door. One of the soldiers gave him an encouraging look, come on, it's okay; he stopped and looked back but could only see the sergeant, who looked bored, perhaps even irritated, by the old man's hesitation. He couldn't see the other two men: they were lying down again, face up, their hands across their chests. He took a deep breath, crossed the threshold, and dragged his feet with little steps down the corridor. He heard the door closing behind him, the key turning in the lock, and the soldiers' heavy boots striking cement. They took him to the washroom, where he stood as long as he could under the shower. Then they gave him those homespun clothes, and the old man smiled as he stroked the coarse material, what's he running like that for, that poor young man?

He had chosen one of the emptier compartments, see, there's only one peasant inside, and mumbled good day to the other man, who was busy pushing a wicker basket as far as possible under a seat, and who answered with a mumbled greeting of his own. Afterwards the young man came in with the briefcase and a bunch of flowers. The peasant eyed him suspiciously until the young man fell asleep with his mouth open and his head propped against the overcoat hanging by the window. The old man also fell asleep. When he awoke, the young man had gone and the peasant was rummaging in his basket. He took out something wrapped in several pieces of cloth: at first it looked like a child—or so he thought, for a moment—but how could it be a child, you don't keep a child under your seat. It was a fish as big as a baby: the peasant looked at it tenderly, then covered it again in its dirty rags and put it back where it had been before. A woman and a tall man with a moustache entered the compartment. They looked like foreigners, but the old man couldn't tell Italian and Spanish apart. He'd learned a little English in prison and knew some French—enough to read a paper, anyway. They were Italian. The peasant looked at them distrustfully, even a little scornfully. The old and the young man exchanged a glance of complicity. The ex-convict gave a faint smile, but the peasant looked away without returning it.

The Italian lit a cigarette, blowing the smoke in rings and pointing them out playfully to the woman, but she didn't seem too thrilled. Only when the man said something and pointed to the emergency brake cord did she finally deign to smile. He rose to his feet and reached up to the cord, sealed with wax, no, the woman said, *ti prego*, what on earth are you doing? growled the peasant. The Italian sat down again: he'd only been joking, and he smiled at the other two. The old man returned the smile and was about to enter into conversation with him—that is, to say a few words in French—but he noticed the peasant's look of disgust and gave up the idea. Besides, he didn't like the *moustachu* either. He wedged his neck in the back of the seat and closed his eyes. A bluish light where rats were scrambling around. The *moustachu* was laughing, at the end of the hall. "So you wanted to escape? You thought you could get away, you dirty old pig?" He was crawling on all fours among the rodents, which were gnawing at his thighs and calves. Where was there to run to? Outside there were cacti, only cacti as far as the eye could see. "I wasn't trying to escape, I swear." And then the *moustachu* came closer and kicked him in the cheek. When he came to his senses, he was back in the cell. He saw the tall rusty door full of scratches, hope sprouted again in his soul, it couldn't last much longer, they'd come sooner or later, today or tomorrow. And the others thought the same, encouraging each other as they waited. After they released Milescu, the guy with the organization to help communists, the waiting was even more difficult. "Why did they let that one go? Why should they release someone like that, who had been poking fun at them—because that's what he was doing, wasn't he?" "Why do you think he was poking fun at them?" the student asked. "Maybe, you know, he really thought they would need to be helped, someday." "Oh yeah, he took pity on them," Fredi chuckled. "He just felt *so* sorry for them! Come on, let's be serious." The old man was silent, although it was he who had started the conversation. He said nothing, or occasionally mumbled a few words, his eyes fixed blankly on the iron door that had opened one fine morning to reveal the sergeant. Guessing immediately, before they called his name, he stood up and breathed in as deeply as possible, to calm the beating of his heart. He didn't dare look at the others, or say anything to them. He made a gesture with his arm, only half a gesture really, and then, prodded by the sergeant's orders, crossed the threshold and followed the two soldiers down the corridor, behind the rhythmic hammering of their boots. The sergeant brought up the rear.

After the shower, they took him into a room where a captain gave him a little speech. Then they gave him his papers, his watch, and a travel permit. The station was close by.

"ARE YOU GOING TO THE STATION?" THE WOMAN ASKED ME, AS she wiped her knife on a piece of bread. The fish were lying inert, probably dead.

"Yes, to the station." And I moved my arms like engine pistons, while rhythmic panting and whistling sounds came out of my mouth. The bunch of flowers slipped from my lap, I bent down to pick them up and hit my head against the metal bars behind the driver. I let out a long hiss, a sad hiss; the woman could control herself no longer and started to laugh. I laughed too, like an idiot. The woman's long-suppressed laughter now came out in guffaws, and the other passengers began to laugh too, ha ha ha, and the woman dropped the bag with the fish and was almost choking.

"Yes, to the station," I said, between two guffaws, "I have to go to an ichthyology congress"—and I stood up and took a bow, removing my top hat with an elegant gesture. Then the driver burst out laughing. The bus started to zigzag, the woman toppled down on all fours, other passengers lost their balance as well, my top hat flew from my hand, and I only just managed to grab the bars in front of me to stop myself from falling. The driver avoided the accident. After the big scare, people got back to their feet with a sigh of relief and turned their anger against me: they looked at me suspiciously, some even hostilely. He should get off, one voice said. Yes, that's right: make him get off! This bus isn't going to the station. Off! Off! Get off! "It's his fault we all nearly croaked," said the pregnant woman.

Everyone was against me. What could I do? The driver opened the door, the passengers were screaming and shouting: I obeyed and got off. Once on the pavement, I realized that I no longer had my hat or even my jacket, and that my shirt was torn in several places. The bus drove off again. Without me. Now I'm sure to be late, even if for some reason—someone pulling the emergency brake, for example—the train had to stop in open country and the driver hasn't been able to make up the time. The bus moved away slowly, as if to make fun of me alone there on the pavement, wearing only my shirt. I looked around: people were walking calmly, each minding his own business; no one was taking any notice of me. No one stopped to say a word, to ask me what had happened, why the bus had dropped me off between stops, whether I was feeling ill, whether I needed something.

So, I made up my mind: I took off my shirt and removed my trousers, until I was wearing only my underpants and the black T-shirt that Magda had embroidered with the gold letters LOVE. I breathed deeply, once, twice, and ran off in pursuit of the bus, determined to catch up and even overtake it. I ran quite fast, I had a very elegant scarf. Passersby stared at me, puzzlement in their eyes: some probably thought they were watching a long-distance race and turned to look for the other runners. I gained a lot of ground, coming within thirty yards of my goal, and soon everyone was able to see a young athlete who had the courage to take on a bus. I accelerated some more, until just a few yards separated me from it. Of course, the driver could see in his rear window the athlete's dizzying progress. Whether the passengers were egging him on or he was acting on his own initiative—it's well known that bus drivers are very ambitious—he decided not to pull in at any more stops. But this immediately won me fresh support among those who had been waiting in vain, since they were obviously now infuriated by the driver's behavior. Some, as fanatical as I, gradually unburdened themselves of their clothing as they ran after the bus; others shouted and cursed in protest at this blatant violation of traffic regulations. The driver was furious that he couldn't gain a decisive lead. At one set of traffic lights, I even drew alongside the bonnet of the vehicle, turned my head and thumbed my nose at the man behind the wheel. From then on he didn't even stop for red lights: policemen blew their whistles at him, other motorists stopped in amazement to watch the spectacle, and then a dark-green bus rolled out of a side street like a tank—or perhaps it actually was a tank, so little did it matter in that mad race.

Who was to blame?

He went to the window, opened it and took a deep breath. For a while now he hadn't been hearing what Maria was saying, or anyway no longer understood what she meant. She continued to grumble at him while he looked calmly out of the window at the roses quivering in gentle gusts of wind. She'll get over it, as she always does. The important thing was to keep from answering back, not to put up the slightest argument in his own defense—that would make it worse—or to make any reply that betrayed annoyance on his part. Just wait for her to finish her long list of accusations and reproaches, then turn to her and smile, like that, as if nothing had happened: how pretty you are, M., and how good to me!

"You ass-kisser, you spoiled brat!" Little by little her brow would smooth out, her voice soften, and as she realized she was losing steam she would try to remain severe a while longer, or else resort to using a weapon that she had no idea how to handle: irony. That was always the most difficult moment in one of their fights, for the simple reason that he felt like laughing when she sharpened her voice to be more biting; it was dangerous feeling, because there was the risk that she would think he was making fun of her and lose her temper all over again. "Go now," she said, in a lighter tone of voice, "go or you'll be late." He shrugged to control his eagerness, his desire to get dressed and escape there and then. The woman drew closer to him and started to caress his hair: why are you so horrid? He took her in his arms but she protested: no, seriously, don't you realize you'll be late? He sulkily looked for his clothes, dressed with haste, and without saying a word opened the door and left. He went down the steps two or three at a time, lacking the patience to wait for the elevator. "Get a taxi!" Maria shouted after him, "and don't forget to buy some flowers."

"I like flowers too," said the woman next to me, and this time she smiled to the driver or his leather-covered back. Then she stood up and leaned forward to whisper in his ear the names of all manner of drugs and exotic plants. He looked around for a few moments before quickly turning the steering-wheel to take a curve: the passengers lost their balance; the woman in black—she had to be a pharmacist—landed in my arms, which opened in the nick of time and then quickly closed in an embrace that continued long enough to suggest something to her, or perhaps it was simply that she didn't like me, perhaps she found the sight of me unbearable, although she didn't need to scream, to tear herself away like that and, without so much as a warning, slap me in the face. As the other passengers got angry with me, I tried to explain that I would miss the train, that I needed to go to an ichthyology congress—and, hearing that word, they became so furious that I was forced to get off the bus. The driver was probably ecstatic.

What was I to do? I had lost the bus, which I could see speeding away, and I risked never finding M. again. I couldn't imagine that she would stand on the platform waiting for me. I began to run. After about a hundred yards I bumped into a rather plump woman: the collision threw me off balance and I very nearly fell. You clumsy oaf! I didn't answer her and started running again, without ever thinking that I could get a taxi. It's true there weren't any around, and no more buses passed by. In fact, the street was blocked because of the terrible accident: a bus turned over on its side, the driver was dead (you don't walk away from that kind of thing!), and I felt sorry for him; it wasn't his fault that some pharmacist had shouted out of the blue that someone was feeling her up. That's exactly what she said: she was a vulgar, probably hysterical woman, a nasty piece of work, pretty ugly and fat, very fat and unattractive, why the hell would anyone feel her up? She had some fish and a loaf of bread in her string bag.

"I didn't see anything," I said. "Or maybe you think I'm guilty? I'm sorry, really I am, but you don't understand that I wanted to help her, that I only held her to stop her from falling. The driver braked suddenly, too suddenly, and we were all thrown off balance. Until then I'd been sitting there, on the seat behind the driver, quietly telling him from time to time that I was in a hurry, that I didn't want to miss the train, you must have seen that."

"Are you going to the station?" the woman next to me asked, in a voice that came out of her lips like a long thin wire.

"Yes, and I'm in a big hurry—although I've heard that the train's running late, someone pulled the emergency brake and the train stopped in open country or by some kind of forest, I'm not exactly sure. You can imagine how long it's taken to find out which car and then which compartment the cord was pulled in, to carry out all those investigations—an old man had begun to feel ill, because of his heart—and to write up their report. But the engineer, who's a very ambitious type, might make up the time anyway; still, I can't risk it." The woman nodded her approval. So, it was a conversation like any other where people talk to each other on the bus. God gave us a tongue, after all.

What can they blame me for?

I bought a ticket and fought my way up to the driver, to ask him to go faster. Sure, you're not allowed to talk to the driver while the vehicle is in motion, to distract him by asking questions, but please believe me that I didn't insist, except at the beginning when I gripped the bars separating us—just think:

there was a window as well—and told him that I was in a real hurry, that I'd seen the bus at the stop and had run to catch it, with a bunch of flowers in my hand and the tails of my coat flapping behind me, and people had turned to look at me with astonishment or indignation, and at the very moment when the bus's wheels started to turn I'd made a desperate leap on to the first step and grabbed the handrail. I'd been lucky.

HE LAY WITH HIS EYES SHUT LISTENING TO THE MURMUR OF THE waves. The sand was no longer so hot beneath him anymore, and the sun had probably hidden in the blankets of cloud: he could no longer feel its talons. Magda had left, or perhaps never come, and he no longer wanted to think of her. He opened his eyes to look at the children who just before had been playing with a bus, but he couldn't see them, the beach was almost deserted, the sky had clouded over and driven most people away. He propped himself up on his elbows, as after a long sleep; the sea had become white with little waves racing to the shore. He lay back again, spreading his arms wide, and remained like that, crucified on the sand, watching through his eyelashes the ever thicker, ever darker clouds. Perhaps it was going to rain. Maria was standing by the window; the wind was shaking the roses and raising a whirl of dust over the paths. "It's going to rain," she said sadly. He was trying to connect the segments of rail, to make the curves fit together, when he heard the woman's voice, opened his eyes, and saw her left thigh protruding from her half-open dressing-gown. "It's going to rain," she repeated with a sigh. The train wasn't working properly, and anyway it was too silly to be playing with model trains at his age.

"You're a big boy now." Maria was trying to be nice and stroking his forehead. She had squatted down beside him, her dressing gown opening to reveal the wonderfully fine skin on both her thighs; he loved to run his cheeks along them. "My darling M.," he cooed, and she purred like a huge cat; his caresses were more and more eager, his tongue a hot snail climbing velvety columns, and his hands dug more and more eagerly into Magda's flesh. My darling M., dearest, dearest M.

From the table, a puzzled Cuculina watched the thrashing of the two bodies as they came together and apart in a slow, ritualistic struggle. When the movements became more violent, accompanied with groaning or even bellowing sounds, grunting or growling, the bird took fright and tried to climb onto the windowsill. It spread its short wings and jumped, but fell down the wall: the sky had glistened blue through the pane for only a moment, then disappeared. The poor chicken! "Why do you keep that chicken in the house?" he asked. Maria didn't answer and continued to dress: first her black silk nylons, which she slowly pulled onto her outstretched and slightly raised legs, so that he could no longer control himself and sank his fingers into her flesh once more. She smiled, without looking at him.

He had opened his eyes again: the clouds seemed to be even thicker. It'll rain for sure, he said to himself, and he thought with pleasure that he would be left alone on the beach, no one would dare to stay, except him, there, crucified, facing the sea. No one. Only he—because now he knew.

"Come on, get up, or you'll be late again." Leaning over him, M. gently stroked his forehead and cheeks; he could feel the woman's fingers, her warm breath as she gradually brought her mouth closer to his face. He didn't open his eyes. This allowed him to prolong her caresses, until M. grew bored or found the position too uncomfortable. Anyway, he waited a few more moments, as it sometimes happened that she would lie on the bed again, beside him, and he could take her in his arms, feel her large warm breasts, glue his whole body to her; the woman let herself be embraced, and so as not to be entirely passive, fondled his hair or the head he had buried between her breasts. "That's enough: you'll suffocate if you go on like that," M. said, pulling herself away, but he pretended to be still sleepy and clung to her large white body, kissing it at random, insatiably, plunging his face into her chest, sniffing her all over. "Come on, get up." Her voice now sounded firmer, so he gave up and tried the final trick of turning over. Then Maria became annoyed and pulled the bedclothes from him, tickled the soles of his feet and—when that proved insufficient—began to take off his pajamas; he kicked about and finally jumped out of the bed—it was too late, really, Magda would get angry again and punish him. He put on his clothes, gulped down some coffee, which was cold now, picked up the briefcase that he always prepared the night before, and turned towards Maria, still in only her dressing gown, standing and waiting at the window. She didn't let him kiss her again and pushed him away with both arms. "Go on, stop wasting time. And don't forget the flowers. They're on the veranda." His classmates used to make fun of him for bringing flowers every day to the schoolmistress. Flowers again, teacher's pet?

He took the flowers and broke into a run. Ion mumbled something, but he paid no attention. The bus was already at the stop. He ran flat out, holding the briefcase in one hand and the flowers in the other, but he didn't manage to catch it.

He waited for the next one. He turned round as he stepped onto the bus: Maria was probably somewhere standing at a window. He got a ticket and took up his position behind the driver. He liked to sit there, to look at the man with the cap and leather jacket turning the wheel and confidently pressing those buttons; it all fascinated him. He took his eyes off the driver only once or twice during the trip: when they passed the window with a little bird inside a large golden cage, or the garden gnome or the gas station. Otherwise, he kept staring at the precise movements of the bus driver; some of the drivers were agitated by the boy behind them watching their every move, eyes bulging, but most got used to it and even spoke to the kid from time to time. "You're late again, kiddo. A bit too much sleep." He smiled happily, or—to make himself seem more important—asked the driver to go faster. "Please step on it, I have a test today." To which the driver replied, "Kid, you're like that hare that got in a race with a tortoise. You know what a tortoise looks like?" "Of course I do!" "Well, that's you: the hare that's had a good sleep and now has to race to catch the tortoise." "Except that I'm not racing; I'm sitting on a bus." "Stop trying to be a wise-guy! Say, what's your teacher's name?" "Magda—Magda Cristescu." "And is she beautiful?" The boy was silent. "Tell me, is she beautiful, this Magda?" "Yes." "Is she a blonde?" The driver had large hairy hands and a moustache. "Well, is she a blonde?" "Yes. She has long hair." "No kidding!" the driver said in mock surprise. "You'll have to introduce me to this Miss Magda of yours."

Then they replaced Miss Magda Cristescu with another teacher called Costescu, Maria Costescu. He took her flowers too, but not so often. "Why did they replace her?" the driver with the moustache asked. The boy shrugged his shoulders: I don't know, he didn't know, how could he know? "And is the new one as beautiful?" He didn't answer. The driver braked and swore at a cyclist who had shot out in front of him and nearly been run over. In fact, the bus did hit him, and the cyclist fell over together with a few fish he'd been carrying in his seat rack. The driver got out when a policeman appeared on the scene. He got out too, with the bunch of roses that he held like a candle, and the briefcase under his arm.

"Hey, mister, your fish are escaping!" The cyclist was not moving: a thread of blood was trickling from his mouth. He opened his eyes. It had not started to rain yet. He heard someone tiptoeing on the sand, stopping a few inches away from his head. His eyes were still closed. Magda was more beautiful than Maria, but why should he tell that to the man with the moustache. What was it to him? "You don't want to tell me, eh?" A hand grazed his forehead and eyelids: he managed to stop himself trembling; it was probably Maria, late again. Slender fingers stroked his cheeks and lips, chin and neck, then moved down to his chest; now there were more hands, two women's hands, but he still had not opened his eyes; there were four hands, twenty fingers; it wasn't important, it was late. Too late.

OF COURSE, IT HAD ONLY SEEMED TO BE HIM—HE WAS SO FUNNY-looking, holding that bunch of flowers!—but in fact he didn't even look like him. She tried to make a mental picture of his face, but all she could see were his anxious eyes. No, these were not his eyes. She searched her handbag and took out a cigarette. The arm of the man opposite arched over to offer her a light; she accepted it and thanked him with a nod. She drew deeply on the cigarette, her head bent back slightly, and blew the smoke towards the window. Then she rewarded the *moustachu* with a smile, which he returned at once. But his servile waiter's smile, routine and automatic, annoyed her even more: his eyes shone for a moment, his moustache moved and the white stripe of his teeth appeared beneath it. The woman smiled again, to see the effect on him, but she didn't realize that now her own smile looked forced. This time, in fact, the man smiled without show-ing his teeth, then looked at her with some surprise as she quickly put the cigarette in her mouth and drew on it twice. He's not such a fool after all! The man looked at her intensely for a few seconds until she turned her eyes away: the plain outside moved slowly, like a huge lid set in motion by invisible subterranean mechanisms. She took another puff and switched her gaze to the peasant, who was sleeping with his mouth half-open, but not snoring. Perhaps he wasn't even asleep, or had just woken up but not yet decided to open his eyes. The old man in the other corner was also looking at the peasant, or perhaps just staring into space: it was hard to tell, because his eyes were not visible to anyone.

The peasant bent down and felt the basket under his seat. The looks of his fellow-passengers must have bothered him a little, or else he was doing it on purpose. He too was playing his little role. The man with the moustache was very attentive to what the peasant was doing: not only did he check that his basket was safe there, beneath the seat; he rummaged inside with one hand—the other resting on his lap—and concentrated very hard, as if he was counting eggs.

Now everyone was looking at the peasant, who was probably happy to have aroused so much interest, however exaggerated. The woman stubbed out her cigarette in the ashtray beneath the window, and the *moustachu* leaned forward to whisper something to her. She nodded her agreement, then made an evasive gesture that might have meant: how should I know? Outside, the plain continued to turn slowly.

Eventually, he too must have understood that at some point things can't be fixed, that there's no going back. Anyway, there was no sense continuing the torture of this crazy shuttling back and forth. What's gone is gone! It's over.

The woman felt very proud of her inner strength: she was much stronger than him—that was for sure. She threw out her chest and sat cross-legged, allowing her short skirt to rise up over her large, powerful thighs. She took another cigarette from her bag, and in a flash the man with the moustache was extending his arm. The sea had acquired a whitish tinge, the color of seagulls or perhaps a little duller. She glanced out of the corner of her eye at the tall man seated beside her, then took another puff on the cigarette. The sea was giving out a long muffled sigh. The man turned his head and smiled in a way that showed his white teeth. Then they went straight to the station.

When the ticket-collector came in, the peasant jumped and looked around sleepily. He began to look for his ticket, searching all his pockets, and eventually found it in his basket. The old man presented a travel permit. The official took another step and held out his hand for the other tickets. He wasn't wearing a railwayman's usual cap, and his dark blue clothes looked almost like a disguise: he had fine features, a high forehead, and very white hands untouched by manual labor. The woman wanted to hear him speak and asked whether the train was running late. He was probably used to having to give people a good impression, even to his intriguing male and female passengers with an interest in physiognomy, because he immediately began to explain in great detail why the train was running late, and to add a host of fatuous remarks about the engine driver and Pamfile and even something about a tortoise. All this time he kept his eyes on the woman's legs and paid no attention to the other passengers; the *moustachu* was the only one to receive an occasional glance. The woman finally held out her hand for her ticket and, unceremoniously cutting him short, thanked him for the information. The collector returned her ticket regretfully and backed out of the compartment, his eyes still glued to her thighs. "Horny bastard," the woman muttered, with a smile to the *moustachu* who wanted to know everything the collector had been saying. She told him in a few words: what amused him most was the story about the tortoise. He took the woman's hand and kissed it tenderly.

The peasant had nodded off again. The old man too had closed his eyes, but the continued murmur of the others' voices prevented him from falling asleep. There's too much chit-chat in this world, he said to himself as he turned over onto his other side; the bed creaked and he heard the others stifling their laughter. Fredi was probably telling them a joke: they laughed like kids at night in a boarding school, burying their heads under their pillows so as not to make too much noise. Then Fredi's voice started up again, a thick raucous voice, and the men were all ears. This time the laughter was even louder, a cross between barking and croaking. He broke into a run: the ground was soft under his feet. He hurtled down a slope, with the croaking somewhere in the distance behind him, and came to a garden where a man was bending down and cutting roses with a large pair of shears. It was quiet there. A bluish light covered everything like a fog. At the bottom of the garden, a woman in black was holding a little boy in her arms. He tiptoed towards her along the gravel path. The man with the shears seemed not to notice him and went on working quietly. He took another ten steps, then stopped, confused: what was he doing here? If they asked him who he was or where he was from, what would he say? The woman stood up, confidently taking the child to her breast, and walked up the few steps to the veranda. The man who had been cutting the roses straightened up, a bunch of flowers in one hand and the shears in the other. He was very tall. He too headed slowly and deliberately towards the veranda. At that moment a chicken appeared from behind a bush. The rose-cutter climbed the steps to the veranda and disappeared, whereupon the chicken ventured out onto one of the paths and from time to time pecked at the gravel. Everything was quiet: all that could be heard were the fowl's tiny steps and the sound of its pecking. It was so quiet! He was all but holding his breath. His forehead was damp, the roof of his mouth dry. Why should he be afraid? He'll say he's lost, and thirsty, yes, just a glass of water and he'll be on his way. He edged nervously towards the veranda steps, frightening the chicken and sending it off to hide in another bush. He went up the steps—the door was ajar—and crept inside. No one was there. He saw a second, closed door, through which came sounds of moaning and panting, as if there was a fight going on. Unsure what to do, he looked around and was about to leave when he noticed some freshly cut roses on a table. He picked them up and resolutely walked down the few stone steps. Not stopping to look back, he leaned gently forward and began to take longer strides; the bunch of flowers hanging from his hand came within inches of the pavement. He could hear his soles echoing on the cement. There were steps behind him. He stopped. Then the sergeant's voice: "Come on, get going. What's got into you?" A shout rang out somewhere. He turned his head and saw a mixture of fury and surprise on the sergeant's face. "Get going, damn you, get going!" He started off again.

They took him to quite a bright room, where an officer, a captain, sat at a table before an open folder, a heap of papers and a pen. He took a deep breath and began to smile. "You're pretty jolly today," the captain said, getting to his feet. Another two men, in civilian clothes, came in and joined them. They looked at him and spoke to each other in a whisper, then leaned over the table and rummaged through the papers in search of something. His feet were hurting: they felt swollen, and a shooting pain in his left knee forced him to lean to one side. On his neck, the hot claw wouldn't spare him for a single moment. He stopped and carefully placed his trunk on the asphalt. He took out a large dirty handkerchief to wipe his neck and forehead, and his neck again. It would be stupid to let fatigue grind him down now of all times. A bluish light covered him and his ears began to ring; he curled up more from fear than from pain. The woman looked at him with surprise in her eyes, and motioned to the *moustachu* to look at him as well. He must be feeling ill. The Italian jumped up at once, as the old man collapsed in the middle of the compartment. One of his arms rested on the knees of the startled peasant, who stood up—or rather tried to stand up—and knocked his shoulder against the Italian's head as he was bending over to pick the old man up. The peasant let out a curse and struck out at random—but the blow hit the *moustachu* right on the chin, causing him to turn round sharply and mutter something in his own language. The peasant hit him a second time. His adversary was quite strong, however, and although the Italian hadn't expected such violence from the peasant—or perhaps for that very reason—he responded by pummeling him in the stomach. The peasant, his leg immobilized by the weight of the old man, lost his balance and fell, which made it easier for the Italian to deal him a blow to the ear that caused him to cry out. Arms flailing, the woman shouted at the ongoing male brawl. The peasant summoned what was left of his strength, pulled his leg out from under the old man's body, and threw himself at the Italian's neck while the man was still off balance from the punch he'd just landed. The Italian collapsed, while the woman, now really frightened, gave another shout, turned towards the emergency brake cord and hung from it in desperation. As the train came to a halt with a long loud whistle and a screeching of brakes, she was thrown in among the three entangled bodies. Recovering a little from the blow, and feeling that he was suffocating under the weight of their bodies, the Italian man tried his best to get to his feet. The woman, hysterical, gripped the peasant's hair tightly; he struggled to free himself and kicked out with his feet—or rather, his knees—at the man on the floor beneath him. The old man was completely crushed.

The door opened and a police officer surveyed the scene in bewilderment. The woman was screaming at the top of her voice, with her hands buried in the peasant's hair; the others were gasping and groaning. The peasant managed to twist himself around—aided by the Italian's efforts to get to his feet—and struck the woman in the face with the back of his hand. She fell on her back and hit her head against the window: blood spurted from her nose and mouth, the captain stepped into the compartment, and the figure of the ticket-collector appeared over his shoulder. The woman was now lying on the floor with her feet in the air, showing her rose-colored panties, and in her tightly clenched fingers she was holding a tuft of the peasant's hair.

The Italian man finally pulled himself up at the very moment when the policeman was stepping aside to allow the ticket-collector to enter, so that it might have seemed as though they were about to pounce on him. Pushed into a corner, the peasant stared at the newcomers without trying to make sense of what was happening. The officer took the Italian by the arm and said a few words to him, whereupon he replied in Italian with a furious gesture towards the peasant.

"What's going on, gents?" the ticket-collector asked calmly, with a hint of mockery in his voice. The Italian continued to speak excitedly, accompanying his words with gestures that he tried to make as eloquent as possible. Then they all turned their eyes to the old man's motionless body and helped the officer to pick him up. "Bring some water," the captain said. "Water!" shouted the ticket-collector, and a minute later a man claiming to be a doctor, or perhaps it was the ticket-collector, said that it was difficult to make anything out in all the commotion. Some splashes of water and a few slaps brought the woman back to her senses. The ticket-collector attended to her, while the doctor leaned over the old man's body and took his pulse. "He's not dead," he said in a high-pitched voice. The Italian started: "*Morto?*"—"Not *morto*," the doctor said with irritation, "but what the hell's been going on here?" The peasant was sitting in a corner with his eyes on the ground; the woman was whispering with the ticket-collector, who was almost holding her in his arms, or anyway seemed very concerned about her fate.

The doctor asked everyone to leave the compartment. "There's not enough air," he said. Even the policeman who had accompanied the conductor to draw up a report wasn't allowed to stay. "Out! Out!" the doctor insisted. The peasant took his basket with him: he wasn't going to leave it there, after all, who knows what might happen? The woman and the ticket-collector were the last to leave.

With an air of self-importance, the doctor took a vial from his bag, skillfully cut through the top, and moving towards the window where there was more light, drew the clear fluid up into a syringe. The old man's face was still swollen, and drops of water were trickling from his moist hair. A bluish light bathed the garden, concentrating itself especially around the woman's majestic body; the child in her arms looked quite big, so it was strange to see her holding it like a baby. The pain in his legs had almost disappeared, but he was thirsty. He ought to go and ask her for a glass of water. He didn't dare: the child had grown and now looked like a man in the prime of life, dressed in his officer's uniform and sporting a moustache. The table stacked with papers lay between them, and again he felt dizzy.

The doctor studied the old man's face and for a moment thought he was moving his eyelids. He turned to the captain, who was pacing nervously; the others had done their duty and left. "It's not that serious: he'll get over it." The captain gave a quick laugh and mumbled something, but the doctor didn't understand: "What did you say?"

There were no flowers. Only cacti, as far as the eye could see, cacti of every size and every shade from green to yellow. They had grown so close together that not even rats ventured to squeeze between them. He didn't dare move. Again he felt their mouths and little claws as they tried to clamber onto him, but he didn't move. The doctor tapped him on the cheek, a bluish light flooded the room, and his eyelashes fluttered. "Come on, wake up, that's enough now," the doctor said, more for the captain's benefit, who had come closer with an enigmatic smile on his lips: it was hard to tell whether the smile expressed compassion or contempt. They had pushed him to the ground, rained him with kicks and punches, trampled on him with their boots. Yet he went on resisting. His head felt like a lead barrel and there didn't seem to be enough air. "Hurry up!" the sergeant said between his teeth, and he began to pace again, dragging his boots and holding his hands behind his back. He stopped, spat into the corner with the bucket, and told a soldier to open the door wider: "It stinks to high heaven in here!" Then he turned to the prisoner, who had risen to his feet and was breathing as deeply as possible to calm the beating of his heart. "So, you're getting keen on gymnastics, are you?" the sergeant chuckled to himself; the others were standing upright with their brows knitted—not even the soldier by the door thought it necessary to smile. After putting on his boots, the old man remained bent over for a few moments, then turned his head a little towards the long empty corridor. He tried to mutter something, but all that came out were a few incoherent sounds: he had nothing to say. He raised his left arm to the level of his ear and let it fall again, then buttoned his jacket, stood up, and took a few steps towards the door. One of the soldiers gave him an encouraging look, come on, it's okay; he stopped and looked back but couldn't see the other men, who had lay down again on their beds and were looking up, their hands across their chests.

The ticket-collector came back into the compartment. "How is he?" The doctor shrugged by way of reply and again dabbed the old man's face with a strong-smelling liquid.

A bluish light in which rats were scurrying around. The *moustachu* was laughing at the end of the corridor, arms outstretched, knees bent. "You wanted to run for it, didn't you? You wanted to get away, you little lump of shit." He fell on all fours and watched the other man with fascination, as he seemed to occupy the entire space between the two walls. He could feel the rats teeming all around him. Where could he run? Outside there were cacti, gardens with roses and cacti, women holding uniformed babies in their arms, I didn't mean to do it, really I didn't, and then the *moustachu* came forward and kicked him on the chin, he fell, dropped on his belly trying to catch his breath, but strong hands lifted him up and slapped him in the face. You miserable old bastard!

The doctor slapped him a little harder and the ticket-collector smiled. The compartment door was still half-open; some inquisitive people had gathered outside in the corridor but didn't dare to enter. They annoyed the ticket-collector, who stretched out and shut the sliding door. Then he turned his attention back to the doctor. "Maybe he needs another injection," he suggested. The doctor didn't reply, and with the back of his hand once more slapped the old man's swollen, yellow-purplish face.

He guessed it before they called his name. He stood up and tried to breathe deeply, so that he wouldn't be reminded of the shooting pains that he had felt for more than a month below his left shoulder blade. He breathed deeply to calm the beating of his heart. He didn't dare look at the other men, nor even talk to them. He made a vague gesture with his arm, no more than a semi-gesture in fact, and then, driven on by the sergeant's harsh words, crossed the threshold into the corridor he knew so well. Left-right, left-right-left. He followed the rhythm of the soldiers' boots. The sergeant kept a little behind.

After the shower, they took him to a large, bright room, where a nice captain with a moustache—or, anyway, a captain doing his best to be nice—started a rambling speech, that went all round the houses, giving him advice about the future with a knowing smile; the whole thing was pretty incomprehensible to him. Then they returned his papers, his identity card, his army papers, and a photograph of a child playing cross-legged with a train.

I GOT ON THE BUS AT THE LAST MOMENT. THAT'S LUCKY, I SAID
to myself, as I took out some change to buy a ticket. The ticket-
seller gave me an encouraging smile—she'd seen me before,
thank God!—and I threaded my way through to sit behind the
driver. I kept looking at my watch: I was in a hurry. The woman
next to me, who until then had been looking out of the window,
turned her head and looked me up and down. It made me nervous and I lowered my eyes.

"I'm in a hurry," I mumbled to the driver, who certainly
didn't hear me. The woman continued to stare, as if she were
seeing me for the first time. I peered at her out of the corner of
my eye, not daring to raise my head. She looked like M. She
was much fatter, it's true, but just as pale and also with rings
around her eyes. "Why did you get those rings?" he asked while
she was eating. He said it without looking at her; she seemed to
be sitting with her face in the plate. "Come on, hurry up," M.
said as she got up and went to the window. He glanced at her
and saw her frowning. The chickens! he thought happily, and
he went on slowly chewing his food. When M. left the room,

he took the opportunity to pour himself another glass of wine and gulped some down before returning to the meal. When the woman came back, he still hadn't finished eating. "You'll be late," she said, raising her voice. He smiled and looked in the direction of the window, then at the curved breasts trembling beneath her dress.

"M., is that you in that picture?" he asked with his mouth full, trying to seem as natural as possible, because he'd asked the same question many times before and never received an answer. She didn't reply this time either, but only glanced at the painting of a woman with a child in her arms.

"Get going, or you'll be late," M. said. "And make sure you don't forget the flowers." He went up to her with his eyes begging for a kiss, but the woman didn't yield and pushed him firmly away. She was wearing a long dark dress, which made her skin appear lighter than it was. He opened the door. The woman went out after him, to make sure he wasn't forgetting the flowers. They went down the stone steps together; the gravel crunched under their feet. He turned again at the gate, but still she wouldn't let him kiss her. She held him away with both arms: "Off you go, stop wasting time!"

He strode along with his coat open; the bunch of flowers, carefully wrapped in paper, hung at the end of one arm. The street was deserted. In a courtyard, a man had forced a pig on its back and was preparing to stick a knife into it beneath the gaze of three women in thin silk dresses. Propped against the bare wall of the house next door, a child was sitting on crossed legs and playing a sad, simple melody on a pipe or flute. So absorbed was he in the scene that he didn't notice the dog that had broken loose from its fence until he walked right into it. He stumbled but didn't fall. He crossed the street. A man in a striped jersey, with a kind of top hat on his head, came out of the alleyway of an old building. He broke into a run. The flowers held him up, but he couldn't bear to throw them away. Four more cyclists caught up with him. He saw the bus waiting at the stop and sprinted to catch it. Its big wheels started to turn, the ticket-seller waved to him—too late!—and the door closed.

He couldn't doubt it any longer: he was going to be late. There was no point waiting for another bus. M. would understand. Meanwhile, she might have calmed down, she might have changed her mind. Otherwise, if she's really determined to leave, she can take the trouble to go the station herself. He'd help her carry the suitcase and still buy her ticket—but there's no way she'd catch today's train now. Yes, he'd go back and explain that he made every effort, that he really didn't do it on purpose. He'll go back up the stairs, he won't call the elevator so that it takes even longer, he'll knock on the door, she probably won't be dressed yet. "What's up? Why are you back so soon?" "I missed the bus, really. I ran like crazy, but when I got to the stop the bus was leaving. The door shut right in my face." M. looked at him suspiciously for a few moments, then turned on her heels and went into the bathroom. "Please go away. Leave me alone." He said nothing, staring like a fool at the bathroom door. "Do you understand?" Her voice sounded as though it was coming out of a barrel. "Well, okay, whatever you want . . ." But he didn't leave. He sat on the bed and waited for her to come out. He could hear water running in the bathroom, then her voice: she wanted to know if he'd gone. No, he hadn't gone: he's sitting on the bed and waiting for her. "Please go away!" "Okay, but what about the luggage?" "Don't worry, I can manage." He said no more and went to the window: the sky was a clear blue. "Wouldn't you rather we go to the beach?" he shouted as loud as he could, to cover the sound of the water. M. turned off the tap and he asked her again. Her voice became surprisingly calm, even friendly. "You go first. I'll join you later." "I'll wait for you." "Don't wait for me." "I'll be waiting in front of the refreshment stand, you know the one. Did you hear me?" He rattled the handle of the bathroom door, but it was locked. "Okay," he said, "I'll go and wait for you there." A fairly honorable exit after all.

The beach was a swarm of bodies that spoiled his appetite for bathing. He took off his sandals and walked into the water. Some children were playing with a model train, having set up the rails just a few inches from the high-tide mark. But a slightly bigger wave could come along at any moment, and it was probably this constant danger that excited them more than anything else. At some point, the stationmaster gave the order for a sand dyke to be built: a quarrel therefore broke out when most of the other children indignantly refused to obey. The train seemed to belong to the stationmaster—that is, the one in control of the buttons—and this made things a little more complicated. "It's my train," he said, and no one suggested otherwise.

He sat on the sand beside the children, but did not interfere. His presence disturbed the owner of the train, who agreed to let the game continue despite the insecurity. The others now also suddenly became conciliatory—all because of him. He got up and left.

He went into the water and swam for a long time, ending up more than half a mile from the shore. When he returned, he started to look for M., although he was sure she wouldn't come even if she hadn't left for the station. She would certainly go somewhere other than the place he had told her, so it would be stupid to go searching. But he still walked a little here and there. A woman of rather advanced age was exposing her large flabby breasts to the sun. Two youngsters kissed and stroked each other, until a third came and began to cover them with sand. None of them laughed. He got dressed.

On the steps leading up to the cliff, he stopped at the refreshment stand and asked for a lemonade. The woman serving there had quite a large fish on her lap. He was thirsty and asked for another glass. The woman winked at him and pointed to the fish. Only then did he notice that she was wearing only a short blouse and nothing at all down below.

"Come inside," the woman said. He shook his head and left. He was so hot—almost wilting—that he could barely drag his legs after him as he walked the length of the cliff. He went into a café. There was scarcely anyone there in the cool room, just a couple of sailors drinking beer and talking in whispers. He sat at a table in the corner and ordered a glass of iced coffee. "With a lot of ice!" He rested his head on his hands and thought of M.—not of this M., but of the other one. He saw her in the garden, that evening when—for want of anything to say—he'd explained his theory of anarchism to her. "It's the only solution," he had said, and M. listened with a sad smile because she knew he would leave. The only solution: abolition of the state. "How?" she asked. "Well, first we'll blow up the Telephone Exchange.

I've come to the conclusion that an attack on the primary means of communication . . ."—and they both forced themselves to laugh. From M. to M. The waiter brought the iced coffee. The sailors had brought their chairs closer together and were embracing one another. He sipped the coffee and looked at his watch. "Get going or you'll be late," M. had said. "The train's late, they told me." But he was all on edge. When he tried to kiss her at the door, she pushed him away: "Cut it out: you've got to go." He left, without looking back again. He walked in long strides, bent slightly forward. In a courtyard, a man in a driver's cap was cutting a pig beneath the gaze of three women holding three white bowls. A little further on, a child was playing a flute. He broke into a run, crossed the street, and dodged an old man who was dragging along a suitcase or trunk, the kind that conscripts have. He spotted the bus at the stop and with one last effort managed to catch it. The old man, not in any hurry, was still back there. He took another sip from the coffee: it was nice and cold. The sailors were whispering and touching each other like a pair of lovers. He saw the hand of one on the other's thigh, then on his fly. He paid and stumbled his way to the door. Outside, there was a blinding sun. A huge fish drifted over the trees, chased by what looked like a vulture. He headed for the hotel. M. had left: the key was hanging at the reception desk.

The elevator girl smiled at him as usual. They were alone, and he could have suggested that she come to his room at the end of her shift, in an hour's time. He'd be waiting, but she mustn't be late, because he had to leave a little later to meet someone at the station. That's how one should speak in such situations: as simply and directly as possible. But, of course, without being too crude.

The girl will come and knock on the door; he'll call for her to enter. She has a provocative smile, but a shy way of walking. "Take a seat. It's hot today. Wouldn't you like something cold?" She nods, dropping her chin on her chest, and he opens the fridge. "Perhaps a little whisky on the rocks?" The girl smiles, takes off her shoes, and raising her short skirt a little higher, shows him how tanned she is. "It's normal if you spend so much time by the sea." Then he asks her her name. She doesn't answer and comes closer; she's very short. He kisses her and asks the same question—to say something, to exchange a few words. "Guess," she says, with an awkward, possibly nervous smile. He kisses her again and feels her breasts under her blouse. "I can't guess: there are so many names." He seeks out the zipper on her dress, a little clumsily. All she tells him is her initial: "My name starts with M.," she laughs. "Wait, I'll take it off myself."

He gets up from the bed and goes to the window. It's late, he'll be late. They both dress hurriedly, avoiding looking at each other. "Do you really have to go?" M. asks. "Yes, I must," the man replies dryly. They say goodbye in front of the elevator. He makes as if to kiss her, but she doesn't let him. "Go on, or you'll be late." And she walks off down the corridor.

He gave up taking the elevator. He ran down the stairs two or three at a time.

THE ENGINEER DIDN'T ANSWER. HE PULLED ONE LEVER, THEN another. The ticket-collector said nothing for two or three minutes, after which he started talking again in the same calm and, he liked to think, persuasive tone.

"Look, I'll suggest a simple proof, one that any child could manage. Take the distance between two points: A and B."

"How many miles?" the engineer asked.

"Forget about the miles, that's not what this is about."

"So, what is it about?"

"Hang on, for God's sake, be a little patient."

The ticket-collector took out a sheet of paper and drew a straight line on it. At the two ends he wrote in thick capital letters: A—C. Like that, more or less.

"So, let's say that it's the distance between two towns—or it could be two people, it doesn't matter, the important thing is that it's a distance, a space. Right?"

"Right. So what?"

"Well, now let's say that between A and C, between these two towns—or not towns, two points, you see what I mean?—that here, halfway between them, is point B. That's the middle, the halfway point. And between A and B let's put a point D, and between A and D a point M . . ."

"Why M?"

"Didn't I tell you it doesn't matter?" the ticket-collector snapped. "Why do you have to interrupt me?"

"I can't see where this is heading," the engineer said, and he bent down to look at the speedometer. "We're going at eighty miles an hour," he noted with satisfaction. "You'll see we can make up some of the time we lost."

"Like hell we can! That's an illusion, and I'll prove it to you. Listen. So we have A and C, then B, D, and M, or, all right, P, if you don't like M."

"P for prick," the engineer said with a laugh. "Stop messing around—we'll be arriving soon."

The ticket-collector felt deeply hurt and said no more. Obviously you can't discuss anything with someone like this: he's an idiot, and ill-mannered on top of it. He put the paper in his pocket and looked out through a small side-window.

"I hope you're not angry with me, at least," the engineer said, detecting the other's annoyance. "Really, either you're making fun of me or you take me for a complete fool. I'll listen if you want, but you must know there's no way you can convince me. There's no sense at all in what you're saying. I don't know where you read it, or who put that rubbish in your head. Believe me, it's not possible: it defies every law in the book."

"If you had a little patience . . ." the ticket-collector mumbled, moving closer to the engineer.

"Okay, I'll listen. I swear I won't say another word."

The ticket-collector again took out the sheet of paper and turned it over. With his pen he drew a new line across the length of the paper. At one end he put a capital A, and at the other an even larger Z. In the middle he put a capital M.

"To get from A to Z," he said in a serious, almost solemn tone, "you have to pass through M. Do you agree?"

"Agreed." The engineer was now conceding everything, to keep this madman happy.

"Right. Now—but just a second . . ." And he inserted a point between A and M and called it F. The engineer only just suppressed an obscene completion of the letter.

"F, the halfway point—do you understand?"

"How the hell couldn't I?"

The ticket-collector looked up at the engineer, thinking that he might be poking fun, but then pulled himself together.

"So, to get from A to M you have to pass through F. Is that clear? But to get to F you have to pass through, let's say, C."

"Or D," the engineer said, quite seriously.

"If you like," the ticket-collector allowed. "And to get to C, you have to pass through . . ."

"Through M," the engineer said.

"We already have an M."

"Yes, that's true: we have an M."

"Anyway, it doesn't matter. We'll put another letter, or the same one with a number, M_1, for example. Do you remember geometry? M_1—M_2 . . ."

"I don't remember much," the engineer sighed.

"It's not important. What I'm showing you is simple, as simple as saying good morning. You don't need to know any geometry or algebra or anything. All you have to do is pay attention and give it a little thought."

The engineer looked through the thick window in front of him and frowned. "Hang on a minute, we're approaching the station and all we're doing is thinking about some mathematical demonstration. I'm sorry, but we're going to have to drop it. You can show me some other time."

The ticket-collector again put the paper in his pocket, crumpling it in the process, and silently made for the little door at the back of the cabin.

"I promise I'll hear you out another time," the engineer shouted after him. The other man passed through to the mail car. What a loony guy! the engineer thought to himself as he pulled a lever.

IT ANNOYED ME HOW SLOWLY HE WAS GOING, THAT DRIVER WITH the thick red scarf. I was happy to be sitting behind him, in my favorite place, because I have to admit that I wasn't usually able to: either I found someone else there, most often a woman, or, if I was lucky and the seat was free, after no more than two or three stops a pregnant woman would get on, or an old man dragging a huge suitcase, and then—what could I do?—I ignored them, looked out of the window, tried to move in such a way that they thought I was ill, handicapped, impossible to budge, but it did me no good, in the end I stood up of my own accord, so to speak, as I could no longer stand the terrible psychological pressure—you don't realize what that kind of pressure means!—or, if not, if I gave no sign of life, the woman claimed her rights by appealing to the other passengers, who were more than happy to be presented with the opportunity.

The bus stopped again. So many stops! I looked out of the window: I saw M. on the sidewalk, with a tall mustachioed man, who was leading a peacock on a leash. M. wasn't looking in the direction of the bus, so I couldn't wave to her. I leaned towards the driver, towards the window separating us, and whispered to him to stop. "I want to get off," I said. The driver didn't hear me, or pretended not to hear me. The bus started up again. M. was no longer visible: she'd disappeared into the crowd. Maybe I'd made a mistake and it hadn't been her. Maybe I'd imagined it. Maybe it was just a woman who resembled her, another woman: people sometimes look alike, even women. It couldn't have been her. But I would still have liked to get off. I was going to be late anyway. I preferred to go home—what was the point of going anywhere else? "Stop, driver, please stop." But the driver wouldn't stop anymore, not even at the bus stops. The passengers got very worked up and looked out of the windows on the other side of the bus. What was going on? The woman next to me, who was pregnant, asked me to stop poking my elbow in her belly—if I could help it . . . And to stop fidgeting in my seat. "But what's going on?" "It's a race, between our bus and a young athlete who's trying to beat it. A symbolic race," someone calmly suggested. "I'd like to see as well. Please let me out." "Go, if you want to, but be careful you don't poke me in the belly. Go on!" I squeezed past the belly, but a man who kept standing on tiptoe to see what was happening outside accidentally pushed me back onto the pregnant woman. "You bastard! I told you to be careful." "Please excuse me, I swear I didn't do it on purpose." "You bastard, what if it makes me have a miscarriage?" she wailed. I tried to defend myself: "Really it's not my fault"—but the man pushed me again, and again I fell on top of the woman. "Help! He's crushing me!" she screamed. I grabbed hold of the man who was the cause of my fall and heaved myself up. He turned round and began to shout that I was fondling him. "I didn't mean

91

to, really I didn't. It's just that the lady could have a miscarriage if I land on her again." "Look at that, he's caught up with us!" a woman bawled out, and she began waving her arms in consternation or perhaps joy. What could I say? All I saw were the backs and heads of the other passengers, screaming and shouting and jostling one another by the windows. "He's caught up!" the woman repeated in the same loud voice, and she too resembled M., or rather not M., but M., they all resembled one another. "Let me see for myself what's happening." "What are you pushing like that for, young man?" "I want to see." "There's nothing to see: some loony running beside the bus." "Why's he running?"

She looked so much like M. She had M.'s way of smiling just with her eyes, without moving her lips. He wanted to embrace her. He drew closer to her, with his arms wide apart. "Get going, or you'll be late," the woman said, pushing him away, "and make sure you don't forget to take the flowers." He took the bunch of flowers and smiled at Ion, who was surveying the scene with his hands behind his back: he must have been holding his large rusty shears in one of them. "Get going"—and he left, without looking back. The woman had continued to clutch the green bars and kept looking after him for a long time—or perhaps she was staring into space without seeing him. Neither had she seen it when he stopped in front of a courtyard where a driver was cutting a pig, aided or merely observed by three women in long silk dresses, or when he very nearly tripped over a mongrel that shot out from behind a fence. Then he broke into a run, the bus was already at the stop, he had no way of catching it.

What was I to do? I didn't dare return home. She would have been furious to see me again and would've given me a hard time.

I waited for another bus, and maybe I would have managed to be on time after all if the driver hadn't been so stupid as to get into a race with a madman pretending to be a great athlete. Dressed in a black T-shirt, he was running alongside the bus—and others had started to run with him, whether passersby or people who had been waiting for the bus and been astonished, or infuriated, to see it sail past their stop. This driver's making fun of us, they must have said to themselves. The people in the bus were no less agitated. Many of them would have liked to get off, either because they had things to do or simply because they were afraid, and rightly so. But others entered into the spirit of things and urged the driver to put his foot down and win the race. It was a real circus as they quarrelled among themselves and everyone tried to out-shout everyone else. "Did you see what he's got written on his T-shirt?" an old man with a moustache asked. "LOVE," a woman passenger spelled it out. "He's an athlete of love, a champion," the woman who looked like M. said with a smile. "A great champion," the man said, "a great champion!" The passengers were divided into two camps: some sided with the runner, out of admiration for his courage or simply because they were angry that the driver was skipping stops and making them late for work; the others had it in for the athlete, for exactly the same reasons. "The poor thing," said one peasant, who sat quietly on a seat without taking part in all the commotion. He held a wicker basket in his arms, and every now and then he plunged his large knotted hands deep inside it.

I probably wouldn't have been late and things would have happened differently. That's the truth—I was unlucky. Then the accident happened and a number of people died, including the driver. In the end it was his fault. Why was he driving like a maniac? He ran traffic lights, policemen whistled at him in impotent despair, a tank came out of a side street with a star on its turret—who was to blame? I woke up on the pavement, with a woman in my arms. It felt so good, what did I care about the accident!

"Come on, get up!" M. said, and he mumbled something and buried his face between her large warm breasts. "You'll be late!" He held her sleepily in his arms, and the woman only just managed to extricate herself. She got out of bed and said more severely: "Get up, or you'll be late!"

He turned over, and the woman, exasperated by his stubbornness, pulled off the blankets he'd wrapped himself in. Now he had no alternative: he obviously couldn't persuade her to rejoin him in bed, so he jumped up: you're right, it's late. He dressed hurriedly, drank some coffee that had almost gone cold, and ran down the stairs of the apartment block. In the street he continued to run, the tails of his coat flapping behind him. Passersby looked at him with astonishment or even indignation: where's he running to, as if the devil was after him? In fact the wheels of the bus had begun to turn, the rear door had closed, and the vehicle had slowly pulled away from the stop. He came to a breathless halt.

HE COULD FEEL THE SUN ON HIS NECK, UNABLE TO SHAKE OFF
its searing claw except with the help of his handkerchief. He
stopped, put down the trunk, and looked at the marks that the
handle had left in his palm. Then he took a handkerchief from
his jacket pocket and began to rub his neck, his hairless pate and
forehead, and then his neck again. A passing cyclist knocked
into him with his shoulder. What a funny guy! He was wearing
a top hat, and in a saddlebag there were a few fish and a bunch
of roses. He smiled. The sergeant also smiled, and you couldn't
tell whether this smile was expressing sympathy, indulgence,
or disdain—probably all three at once. Come on, get going!
He looked at the others, who were standing bolt upright with
bowed heads. He put the handkerchief back in his pocket, picked
up the trunk—it wasn't so heavy—and set off again. He walked
with firm steps, trying to fall in with the soldiers. Left, right,
left! Their heavy boots rang loudly and rhythmically.

The others had started to chat, lying on their beds. They
teased Milescu; it was Fredi's favorite way of passing the time.
"So, tell us, old man, how did the idea come to you?" Milescu

said nothing. The student tried to stand up for him, and then Fredi lost his temper and paced around the room. He sat on the edge of his bed, palms obediently resting on his lap, and didn't say a word. "Tell us what you think, why don't you say anything?" Fredi asked. What should he say? He went on looking at the door. He discovered a fresh scratch—or maybe he just hadn't noticed it before. It was straight, as if drawn with a ruler, and it led to the peephole. A railway line.

"Come on, get going!" The sergeant spat in the direction of the bucket and ordered a soldier to open the door wide. The old man pulled on his boots and stood up. The soldier by the door gave him an encouraging look; he hesitated a moment longer, then crossed the threshold of the cell. He stopped and turned around but could only see the sergeant, who looked very bored, perhaps even irritated, by all his hesitation. He couldn't see the others anymore: they were lying on the bed again, face up, hands crossed on their chests. The corridor looked long and empty between the soldiers' shoulders. He heard the door scraping shut, the key turning in the lock, the metal-heeled army boots striking cement.

Another cyclist passed by him. It was hot: he raised his hand to his neck; the sun's claws held his whole head now. He saw a couple of cyclists, a man and a woman. They were pedaling cheerfully in the direction of the station. It was hot, maybe he should take the bus. He stopped and put the trunk on the asphalt, which had already begun to melt. "Hey, what are you doing there? Keep moving." His legs hurt, especially the knees. Whenever he took a deep breath, a knife cut into his side. He couldn't go on: the pain doubled him up, and there was a rat in his stomach.

He collapsed. They picked him up and dragged him to the cell, where they dropped him like a sack at the foot of a bed. Milescu and the student picked him up and helped him to lie down. "They've beaten you good and proper," the student said. A bluish light spread over everything, and he could see roses and lilies through the half-open door. He tiptoed towards it on the path, feeling the gravel beneath his feet. A man stood half-bent cutting roses, with deliberate, almost solemn movements. He took a few more steps and stopped. What if they asked him what he was doing there? He would have to give some answer, mumble a few words, anything at all, just to say something. Speak. What should I say? Everything you know. He broke into a run. A bluish light gleamed at the end of the corridor: maybe a door. He fell. When he tried to open his eyes, a man with a syringe was standing over him. "It's nothing: he's coming round. Nothing serious." The captain gave a short laugh and growled something unintelligible. "What did you say?" the doctor asked.

They weren't flowers after all. Only cacti, as far as the eye could see. They had grown so close to one another that not even the rats tried to squeeze between them. He didn't dare move. Again the wet mouths, and the little claws trying to climb onto him. But he didn't move. A bluish light, a door, a garden gate, the shape of a man among the flowers. Far, far away. His head felt like a lead barrel, and there didn't seem to be enough air. "Hurry up!" the sergeant growled, again starting to stomp around with his hands behind his back. He stopped, spat towards a bucket in the corner and ordered a soldier to open the door wide: it stinks to high heaven in here! Then he turned to the prisoner, who had risen to his feet and was breathing deeply to calm the beating of his heart. The others were frowning as they stood at attention. The old man put on his boots, buttoned his sleeveless jacket, and tried to mumble a few words of farewell, but he couldn't get anything out. Instead he raised his left arm to the level of his ear and let it fall back down. "Come on, move it!" The prisoner headed towards the door, hesitated a moment, then crossed the threshold. When he turned his head, all he could see was the sergeant closing the cell door.

They took him to a large bright room. He went in and took a deep breath. Seated at a table in front of an open file, the captain looked at him with an ambiguous smile, about which it was hard to say whether it expressed a certain indulgence or only disdain. Maybe even pity. Or else tiredness. So many times. Again and again the same gestures.

Then two men in plainclothes joined them.

A bluish light, the rose bushes, the sturdy guy with those huge shears and a woman: the woman with a child. Which child? A man in the prime of life, sporting a moustache, long past childhood. A captain.

"Is he coming round?" The doctor turned to the officer, who was looking at him anxiously. The other two had disappeared, they were no longer needed.

"It's nothing serious, he'll get over it."

A bluish light invaded the garden, concentrating itself especially around the powerful body of the woman with a child. After a while the woman stood up and went indoors. The man among the rose beds also disappeared.

It was quiet: all that could be heard were the tiny steps of a chicken that had appeared from behind a bush, and the sound of its beak pecking at the gravel. Why should he be afraid? He'd lost his way, seen the light and gone in. He was thirsty, a glass of water, nothing else. He approached the steps nervously. At that moment he saw a boy with a towel under his arm come out through one of the doors leading onto the veranda, followed by the same woman dressed in black. The boy wanted to kiss her, but the woman pushed him away with both arms: "Hurry up, it's late. Cut that out!" The boy took the bunch of flowers from the table and went down the steps. The gravel crunched beneath his feet. The chicken had taken fright and hidden in a bush. The woman was a little behind—she too had walked down the steps on to the path—and was watching him take a bicycle from the shed, or, as he called it, the garage: it was also where he kept his toys, the woman smiled, all those trains, buses, streetcars, his father satisfied his every whim, he really spoiled him too much.

He was studying the grazed and calloused skin left by the trunk handle wearily when a cyclist came up behind him and all but knocked him down with his shoulder. The cyclist also managed to keep his balance and avoid falling, but he stopped, turned his head, and cursed the old man, who paid almost no attention and went on calmly dabbing himself with his handkerchief. He's nuts! The old man picked up his case and crossed to the other side of the street, leaving the cyclist to continue on his way; he had a bunch of red roses in the rack behind the seat.

Certainly not!

"Forget the bike for once and take the bus," the woman called out, and she too went to the gate. "Get going, or you'll be late." This time as well the woman wouldn't allow herself to be kissed; he hesitated for a moment in front of the creaking half-open door—Ion really should keep it oiled—and then made up his mind to leave. He walked with long strides, feeling the gaze of the woman clutching the bars at the garden gate on his neck or between his shoulders. He held the bunch of flowers as if it were a chicken he'd bought at the market. He stopped and gaped for a few minutes at the scene in a courtyard. What's he doing? He'll be late, the woman thought angrily. How absentminded he can be! A little later, he tripped over that mongrel. Then he broke into a run, crossed the street, the bus was already at the stop, the old man too thought he'd never catch it and stopped again: this trunk would be fine if it had a proper handle. He took out his handkerchief, as dirty and stained as a dust cloth, and tried to break the grip of the hot claw on his neck. Then he set off again.

He could hear boots striking cement.

I WAS RUNNING, OUT OF BREATH, JUST A FEW MORE YARDS TO THE
bus. At first people in the street had stared at me with astonishment, but then many of them sized things up and, angry that
the bus was skipping stops, started to run beside me. They didn't
all have decorated T-shirts like mine; some had taken off their
shirts and were naked from the waist up, often turning out to
be white and fat like worms. But they were furious, so in the
end victory should come to us, the runners. At a traffic light I
drew alongside the bus, and thumbed my nose at the apoplectic
driver. From then on he didn't even stop at traffic lights and
left policemen blowing their whistles at him in impotent despair; what happened next was only to be expected in a situation
where every traffic regulation was being violated in broad day-
light—the only thing missing was a tank. And, of course, there
were a lot around that day: maybe they were shooting a war
film. A line of tanks was stationed in front of a bakery, and the
soldiers roared with laughter when they saw me: they pointed;
they were very jolly.

"You're lying," M. said, and she split open the belly of a fish, took out its innards, and threw them to Cuculina, who disappeared with them into the garden. He said nothing and went to see what the chicken was doing. Cuculina was fighting with the other fowl, while Ion was waving his long arms, trying to stop them from disturbing the rose beds. "The chickens have escaped," and M. furrowed her brow as she left to reprimand Ion; the scaled and gutted fish jumped off the table and, with the help of its tail, scraped a little way along the kitchen tiles. When the woman returned, he began to laugh and pointed to the fish that was about to slip under the cupboard. The woman laughed too and bent down to pick up the fish by its tail. Then, as if suddenly remembering: "Get going, it's late."

He opened the window after a struggle with the stiff latch. "Why don't you believe me?" "I do believe you, but there's no time left now. Take your briefcase and flowers and go." He came up and tried to kiss her. "How beautiful you are, M."

"Get going, kiss-ass!"

In the end, though, he had to leave. Ion smiled in a strange way, as if mocking him. He left through the gate and broke into a run. He stopped in front of a courtyard where someone was playing a slow melody on a flute. The driver's knife had cut into the pig's throat, and the women were edging towards it with those white bowls the size of washbasins. All three were smiling, while the child, sitting cross-legged against the wall, played on a flute. Tearing himself away from the spell that gripped him each time, he again broke into a run and only managed at the last moment to avoid falling over the dog that darted out in front of him. There was no bus in sight, of course: traffic was stopped because of the accident, and anyway tanks were occupying almost the entire street. He would certainly be late. He decided to head for the streetcar stop, taking a side street to the right, then another. Maybe the train will be late after all. The streetcar came quickly, almost empty. I got on and asked for a ticket to the station. The ticket-seller looked at me sympathetically and held out a pink ticket. I put it in my mouth and started to chew. "It's sweet, isn't it?" "It's very good," I replied. "Shall I give you another?" "Yes." "Also to the station?" "Yes, to the station." "Are you going to meet someone?" I nodded my head to indicate that I was. "What's her name?" I blushed. She gave me another ticket and I chewed that one too; then she gave me another, which she put directly in my mouth—it was green. And another two or three times. "Have you noticed? They're shooting a movie in the streets, all over town." I nodded. My mouth was full of tickets: I couldn't speak. "Tanks," the ticket-woman said, and I put another handful in my mouth. She was a decent woman, without prejudices. The only other person in the car was a peasant, more old than young, who had pushed his wicker basket under a seat. I sat on the bench opposite and chewed my way through the tickets I'd gotten from the woman. She gave me encouraging looks and showed me an older, slightly larger ticket, but that kind was too sweet. Besides, it's not healthy to eat too much of anything.

The peasant bent over and took a bunch of rags from his basket: a baby in swaddling clothes, or no, a big fish, a carp or barbel. He uncovered its head tenderly, then part of its body. That's good, very good—so it doesn't suffocate. It was hot in the streetcar. The ticket-seller pointed the peasant out to me: she seemed to find him amusing. I looked out of the window. A tank was just then entering a hairdresser's, and the hairdressers inside were shouting and waving their scissors and razors. How cheery the town is today! People are running here and there, scattered by machine-gun fire from the tanks, but no one is dying.

"No one's dying, eh?"

The ticket-seller didn't answer; she was munching on a blue ticket. I repeated my question in a louder voice. The peasant jumped and clutched the fish to his chest.

We went on for a long time. The din from the wheels was never-ending, the streetcar didn't stop, probably because of the excitement outside. "What kind of movie do you call that!" I said to the ticket-seller. And I raised seven fingers to her, with a wink.

The peasant was dozing with the fish in his arms. At a particular moment it broke free of its swaddling clothes, jumped down, and came towards me: it had two thin legs without any scales. The ticket-seller smiled.

"How old are you?" I asked the fish in a squeaky voice, I'm not sure why, probably because I thought it sounded better and that it would understand me more easily that way. It gave no answer. It briefly moved its tail and leaped into my arms. The old man was fast asleep, not having noticed that the fish had snuck away: his arms were still half-folded, his head to one side; he was motionless, only his chest still rose and fell gently. He was snoring. I felt happy stroking the fish nestled at my breast. I was on the streetcar heading for the station: I was going to meet someone, or maybe I was leaving, maybe someone was waiting for me. It felt good.

The fish was about the size of a time bomb. I told this to the ticket-seller, who smiled and took a fish the size of a rifle bullet from her own breast; it was greenish and slightly rusty. She flashed it at me and put it back again. My fish had nodded off in my arms: it was sleeping quietly, its blue scales as tiny as a baby's finger nails.

I suddenly realized that I had to get off. I stood up and carefully put the fish back in the peasant's arms; the ticket-seller had fallen asleep too, and I went up to the driver's cabin. He was a tall man with a moustache, dressed in black clothes and wearing a chrysanthemum in his buttonhole. Beside him a peacock was ruffling its feathers. I told him that I was in a hurry and had been going in the wrong direction: I wanted to go to M., not to M., I had just left M.; she was as good as a mother, often rocked me to sleep in the evening, gave me milk; she was a wonderful woman, but you can't stay with your mother all your life, you've got to leave the nest at some point, as they say. Isn't that true? The driver nodded but didn't stop.

"Please stop," I insisted, "I have to go in the other direction, to the station." The driver looked at me and smiled: the white stripe of his teeth appeared beneath his moustache. "I'll miss the train," I said. "I'm in a hurry." He nodded again and pulled a lever. For a long time he didn't pull into any stops. What stops? All that could be seen to our left and right were tanks. A blinding light came from somewhere in front of us and to the side. What am I doing? I got in this streetcar like a fool and now I can't get out. And it was late and I was going in the wrong direction: I wanted to go to M., not to M., I couldn't get along with M. anymore. The driver said nothing. The peacock's feathers had drooped, and it was dozing in a corner. I started to plead with the driver again. "I absolutely must get to the station. You see, I've just received my draft papers." And I blushed. "So, what do you want me to do?" he snapped, again showing the white stripe of his teeth. "Stop the car!" The driver burst out laughing. Between snickers he told me that the streetcar had been standing still for a long time. "Standing still," he repeated, and he began to kick something metallic. "It's not moving, do you understand?" I said that I did. "How do you think it can move? Can't you see what's out there?" "Yes, tanks." "So what do you want?" I want you to open the door. I want to get off, to try to squeeze past the tanks, to break into a run, like that, coattails flapping, briefcase in one hand, flowers in the other, to run, to race to the bus stop without caring about the disapproving looks of passersby—why is he running as if the devil is after him?—to run, to run, to shed my coat, to take off my jacket, shirt, and trousers, to run in the T-shirt onto which M. once embroidered the gold letters: LOVE.

"AND?"

Pamfile lit another cigarette and resumed his story, accompanying his words with numerous gestures and grimaces that were obviously intended to add some kind of nuance that would otherwise be lost—which would be a pity, wouldn't it?—the ticket-collector nodded attentively, the veins in his neck bulging, clutching the handle of a frying pan.

"And?"

Pamfile raised an arm above his head, slightly bending it in the manner of someone swimming the crawl, and then raised a knee as well—a natural thing to do, because he had been a runner, a sprinter—the ticket-collector stretched his neck still further, apparently attempting a metamorphosis Jupiter himself had only just managed to achieve.

"And?"

Pamfile had already left the starting block, his arms were moving in time with his feet—he was, as it were, fleet of foot, but also fleet of hand—the ticket-collector's neck was now as long as a swan's. Pamfile stopped racing and closed one eye.

"And?"

The race started again, but in slow motion. The left arm rose to the level of the ear, in time with the right knee's ascent to the level of the table, then the right arm and knee also came up, the right knee returning faster to the initial position because Pamfile was running yet remaining on the spot, that is, only pretending to run. That's all we have left: to simulate. The ticket-collector brought a finger to his lips; the other man squinted and twisted his mouth, in mimicry of a superhuman effort.

"And?"

Pamfile hit the knife handle with his knee and made it clatter to the floor. The ticket-collector bent down to pick it up, and then the narrator was forced to start again from the beginning, not quite as wittily as before, and actually the tortoise was asleep, it couldn't care less about Pamfile.

The ticket-collector added a few words, a few phrases, of his own. Pamfile stayed silent: after all, maybe he was right. The ticket-collector left the kitchen and as he crossed the restaurant car put on a grave and distinguished expression. What white hands he had! He began to check the tickets. He took the punch from his pocket and clinked it a few times, as hairdressers do when they're trying a pair of scissors. Then he went into a compartment, punched the tickets there, thanked the passengers, came out and went into another compartment, or rather, no, he'd already been in that one, he hesitated but decided to go in all the same, slid open the door and asked if there was anyone in there who'd just come aboard. The peasant, who was sleeping with his mouth open —or perhaps only pretending to sleep—jumped at the question and began to search for his ticket. The woman beside the window broke off her conversation with the *moustachu* opposite her—it was beginning to flag anyway—and asked whether the train was running late. The *moustachu* was probably a foreigner, but the woman spoke Romanian. The ticket-collector didn't reply at once, but first looked at her suntanned thighs and only then explained, with an overabundance of detail, that someone had pulled the emergency cord, and because of this the train had obviously fallen behind schedule. But the engineer, who's an ambitious, maybe overambitious type, said, well, madam, he'll do everything he can to make up the time. Then he uttered a few words about Pamfile, who'd caught a tortoise, before getting back to the engineer and saying that he knew his job backwards and forwards, without a doubt, but, you see—and here he lowered his voice, making the Italian blink in surprise—he's too pigheaded and, how shall I put it, yes, stupid—pigheaded and stupid. The lady nodded a few times in agreement and held out her ticket. The ticket-collector kept his eyes fixed on her thighs—which irritated her, of course.

"I've been in this compartment before," he said with a dreamy air, "and I think another old man was there in the corner."

The woman shrugged her shoulders, and so did the Italian man. Then the ticket-collector turned to the peasant with an inquisitive look, but he quickly closed his eyes and pretended to be asleep.

"An old man?" the woman asked, reaching out for the ticket that had remained in the collector's impossibly white hands.

"Yes, getting on in years, bald or with his head shaved, I'm not sure which. He had an old trunk instead of a suitcase—the kind they have in the army."

"Ah, a soldier," and the woman took the end of the ticket in her fingers and began to pull it gently. "My ticket," she whispered—and she added: "I haven't seen any soldiers."

The collector gave back her ticket—that is, he let go of it. The woman's thighs showed even more as a result of her efforts to recover the little piece of greenish cardboard.

With evident regret, the railwayman left and slid the door shut behind him.

He'd had enough of sitting behind the driver's leather jacket, getting on his nerves. Now he was the driver. He revved up the engine, put it in second, then third gear, pressed the accelerator all the way down. He looked behind him at the nearly empty bus: only a woman in black, knitting or sewing. Fine, he didn't need any passengers. He began to skip stops, even traffic lights. Traffic cops blew their whistles at him, a police motorbike started chasing him, but what did he care? He sat up in his seat and looked out of the window. Outside, Ion was cutting roses—almost motionless, as if he were praying. The driver decided the bus was a tank and headed straight at Ion. He went through the green railings, and was already crushing the first rose bushes beneath the treads when M. said calmly: that's enough, you'll be late if you don't hurry. Well, he was certainly hurrying. At the last moment he took pity on Ion and swerved to the right, but Cuculina dashed out from behind a bush, he immediately turned left, another chicken appeared, and then to the right again. Ion had begun to yell and M. stood up from her chair: "That's it: take your briefcase and get going!" She came up to him and put her hand on the nape of his neck. The hand felt hot. Ion went on shouting that he'd ruined his rose beds. The frightened chickens were flapping around. He stopped.

"Go on, you'll be late," M. said.

He got up from the chair and tried to kiss her, but the woman firmly pushed him away, with both arms, go away, you've ruined the whole garden. He took his briefcase and went on to the veranda: the flowers were missing from the table.

"The flowers," he said. M. raised her arm and pointed to the garden. Ion was stooping down, the shears hung from the end of his arm, the garden was completely destroyed. The tank could still be heard. He went down the steps. The crushed roses had a strong smell. He rushed to the door, M. shooed him away, get going, and he shut the door and ran.

He stopped in front of the driver's courtyard. The child was playing the flute, the women were standing still with bowls in their arms, the driver had pushed the pig to the ground and raised his knife. The pig made no sound. Again he broke into a run. He crossed the street, turned the corner and reached the road leading to the station. The bus was already at the stop, he didn't need to keep running, he wouldn't catch it anyway. A cyclist passed alongside and shouted something at him. He didn't understand. A soldier with a large green trunk was walking fifty yards ahead; it must have been heavy because he was moving very slowly, scarcely making any progress, there at the edge of the pavement. The cyclist drew alongside the soldier and bumped him on the shoulder, unintentionally, of course. Both men lost their balance, but neither fell over. The one on the bicycle had a striped T-shirt and looked very strong. The soldier was quite old.

The cyclist stopped, dismounted, and swore at the old soldier, who said nothing in return, in fact perhaps he wasn't a soldier at all, he wasn't wearing army clothes. Two or three fish—carp or barbel—jumped from the bicycle's seat rack and tried to run away in the opposite direction. This was lucky for the old man, since the cyclist stopped cursing and went after his fish. The old man took this opportunity to cross to the other side of the street. And here was the happy couple, a man and a woman pedaling their bicycles furiously, their handlebars decorated with flowers, he in a top hat, she in a long dress of black silk. They were singing.

The old man heaved a sigh as he looked at the cuts and bruises left by the handle of his trunk. He felt the sun right on his neck, it was hot; he took out a handkerchief and began to wipe away the perspiration. The cyclist had collected his fish and gone on his way. A schoolboy, with a briefcase under his arm, was running towards the bus stop; there was no way he could catch it—the driver had already closed the doors. He wrapped the trunk handle in his handkerchief and set off again. He walked slowly, with even steps, in no particular hurry. The station wasn't too far, but the trunk felt heavier and heavier. Maybe it would be better to take the bus. Again the sun was clawing into him, into his head. How good it would be to have a hat, or at least a baseball cap. Or a soldier's cap. Or even a helmet. Yes, even a helmet would have given some protection.

Another cyclist passed by. One step, then another. Left, right, left. Now he felt two claws in his neck. He stopped. "What are you doing? Keep going!" He heard the soldiers' boots striking cement. "Why have you stopped?" A shout rang out from somewhere. He turned his head and saw the sergeant's red face. Come on, move, forward march! He started up again, trying to keep the same rhythm as the soldiers. They crossed the courtyard at the back, where the colonel was growing cacti, then entered another building, a hallway, another hallway, and finally a room: large and bright. On a chair inside, a woman was holding a sturdy, almost corpulent captain on her knees. She had a gentle face and seemed to be in pain. The officer was smoking. The sergeant and soldiers clicked their heels and gave the regulation salute. The woman forced herself to smile. The captain stood up awkwardly and approached him. Behind, the woman was sighing with relief and suddenly gave him a cheerful wink. Probably it didn't matter to the sergeant and soldiers, who might have noticed her. "Speak up!" The captain drew closer and stared him in the eyes. "Speak up!" he repeated. Then he made a sign to the soldiers, who grabbed him and took off his jacket and shirt. The woman seemed delighted: she crossed one leg over the other, showing her thick suntanned thighs. They lay him face up on an iron table. He heard two knives rubbing against each other. The woman approached with a bowl the size of a washbasin. He closed his eyes.

A bluish light invaded everything. The storm-ravaged garden was deserted: rose bushes lay broken and crushed, leaving a strong fragrance around them. He breathed deeply and took a few steps; a chicken came out from behind a bush. He went towards the veranda, climbed the steps and approached the closed door. Voices could be heard inside. A woman and a child. "Come on, hurry up! Otherwise you'll be late!" The door opened unexpectedly. He stepped aside, hugging the wall, and a fairly tall boy with a briefcase under his arm came out. The woman followed behind and continued to nag him. The boy went down the steps into the garden. Ion was standing among the rose bushes, hands behind his back. He didn't answer the goodbye wave that the boy gave before closing the iron gate, painted black like the rest of the fence. The boy ran off and the woman returned inside. A bare-necked chicken, with wrinkled pink-and-purple skin, appeared on the veranda. Then he too left the corner into which he had squeezed, and knocked on the door. He went in. The chicken sneaked in together with him. The woman took a few welcoming steps forward and kissed him.

"Look how sweet Cuculina is!" the woman said, taking the chicken between her breasts. The man said nothing. He lay on his stomach, wrapped in the sheets and blankets. "It's late," the woman said. She shooed the chicken from the room and began to dress. First she put on her stockings, which made a nice rustling sound on her thighs, then she stroked her legs and wiggled her hips. He stretched out his arm, but it didn't reach her.

A bunch of roses lay on the veranda table. He picked them up, without a word, went down the three steps, and walked quickly towards the gate. The woman came after him. He turned round at the gate, but she didn't let him kiss her and pushed him away with both hands, get going, she said, stop wasting time.

His head was bent slightly forward as he strode down the street, the flowers hanging from his hand. In a courtyard, a strong-looking man with a driver's cap had pushed a pig onto its back and was preparing to slit its throat, observed by three women with white bowls in their hands. A little boy was playing a flute. He sped up and tripped on a mongrel with a pointed, fox-like mouth that ran straight into him from behind a fence.

He stumbled but didn't fall. He turned into another street. A couple of cyclists, a man and a woman, came out of the alleyway of a house. The man was wearing a top hat, and he seemed familiar. He threw away the flowers. Other cyclists rode up and overtook him. The bus was already at the stop. A boy with a large briefcase under his arm was running to catch it, but there was no way he could make it in time. It wasn't much further to the station. It was getting hotter and hotter.

He put down the trunk, looked at the marks in his hand left by the handle, took out a handkerchief and wiped away his perspiration. A little farther ahead, the sergeant was waiting with a smile; it was hard to tell whether it expressed indulgence, disdain, or both at once. "Come on, hurry up, what are you waiting for?" He looked at the others, who were standing at attention and waiting for the circus to end, Christ, so that they could get going again. The sergeant had lost his patience. "Hey, speed it up, old man, get your boots on!" He put them on, hesitated a moment longer, and got to his feet. For some days he had been preparing a speech for this moment. He coughed. He had more trust in looks and gestures than in words. Why did there need to be so many words? He raised his left arm to the level of his ear, opened his mouth, but couldn't get more than a few incoherent sounds out. He made towards the door, stopped on the threshold, and looked back. All he could see was the pale face of the sergeant, who again smiled in his scornful and indulgent manner. He started up again, trying to fall in with the rhythm of the soldiers' feet. Left, right, left.

Then everything happened all at once: everyone was in a hurry. After the shower, they took him to a room where a captain gave him a little speech, and he was handed back his papers, his watch, and a travel permit.

The station was nearby. He had to keep going on that road where there were only trucks, buses, and bicycles. The cyclists were probably workers coming back from work or the market, because most of them had various kinds of food in their saddle racks. He was in no hurry. He put down the trunk and took out a handkerchief to wipe away the perspiration. It was hot, very hot.

The kid probably didn't have the patience to wait for another bus. He turned back. The old man put the handkerchief in his pocket and lifted the trunk by its handle. At one point, the two looked at each other as their paths crossed.

SHE LOOKED AGAIN AT THE GUY WHO HAD PASSED CLOSE BY
carrying a bunch of flowers as if it were a candle. There was
something defiant in his attitude, and he had given her a look,
as if he knew her and was blaming her for something. Some
kind of moron. With the back of her hand, she stroked the lapel
of the man opposite her. He smiled at her, showing his teeth,
then looked at his watch. The train was due to arrive in a few
minutes, he said in Italian. The woman said something in reply
and looked again at the funny guy with the flowers. She couldn't
find him. No, he wasn't the one. Men can often look alike. An
old man came and sat on a bench a few yards further down. His
head was shaved, his face burned by the sun. She had seen him
somewhere before. She took a cigarette from her handbag, and
the man's arm uncoiled like a spring to offer her a light. She
thanked him with a nod, and the other man smiled. His smile
irritated her: it had from the very beginning, but she had always
tried to ignore it, what did it matter after all? He had a servile
smile, that's what irritated her, although others thought him
polite, a well-brought-up, obliging type. Well-brought-up and

well-built. Yes—and she stroked his lapels again. He took her by the shoulders, and then the train could be heard entering the station. They got into a smoking car, looked for a less-crowded compartment and went into one where a man was asleep, alone. He was wearing bad-quality gray clothes and ankle-length boots, and for luggage had only a large wicker basket, pushed half under his seat with a peasant's usual prudence. They sat by the window and—when the train left—she again saw that man from a few minutes before: he was standing stock-still on the platform, holding a bunch of flowers like a candle or pennant, no, he wasn't the same one, the train was gathering speed and she had glimpsed him for only a second, in profile, with his eyes on the engine, so that she hadn't really been able to make out his features. It couldn't have been him.

The peasant woke with a start, looked around sleepily, and bent down to feel the basket under his seat. The woman looked at him with a certain disdain, but also with understanding. She leaned across to the man who was accompanying her and said something to him in Italian. The peasant glanced at them briefly, then bent down again, pulled the basket out a little, and after rummaging through it frantically, drew out something wrapped in a piece of red cloth. The compartment began to smell of cheese. The Italian delicately stroked his moustache, and the woman again hurriedly said something to him, probably also in connection to the peasant, who now put the cheese back in its place and took out a large object carefully wrapped in several rags. The other two watched him, fascinated. No, it couldn't be a child; the woman was studying his movements, and the tender way he held the bundle of rags made her think for a moment that

it might be a child. But it wasn't a child. The peasant opened
the bundle at one end, and a large fish—a carp or barbel—came
to the surface. The *moustachu* showed his teeth, but this time it
was neither an obsequious nor a conventional smile. The woman
could scarcely stop herself from laughing. The peasant was holding the fish like a baby—in fact, he was rocking it. The Italian
said a few words in a cheerful voice, but fell silent when the
peasant turned and looked at them with suspicion or hostility in
his eyes. He then put the fish in the basket, pushed it as far as he
could under the seat, and rested his head back, closing his eyes.
In a few minutes he was gently snoring.

The peasant woke again when the ticket-collector noisily slid
open the door. The railwayman asked who had got on at the last
stop and made a move towards the couple at the window: he
was obviously attracted to the woman, especially by the thighs
protruding from her short skirt. She had a striking face, fine
hands: the woman wanted to hear him speak and asked whether
the train was running late at all. It was an imprudent thing to do,
because the ticket-collector replied with a longwinded speech
about an old man who had been taken ill, causing someone to
pull the emergency cord, as if he couldn't have just gone into
the corridor and called for help, either from himself, the collector, or from the conductor; the old man had a heart condi-
tion, and some drunk or hoodlum had aimed a slap at this other
passenger who'd been bothering his wife, that is, the drunk's
wife, but accidentally hit the old man instead, so in the end they
just attacked each other and the woman pulled the cord, saying
what else was she supposed to do: let them kill each other? The
way to the corridor was blocked by the old man's body on the

ground, she was seized with panic and saw the emergency cord as her only chance of being saved. The young woman nodded to indicate that she had gotten the point. The ticket-collector wanted to hear what the Italian thought as well, but the poor man had understood nothing and was smiling awkwardly. The peasant sat with his eyes closed: he wasn't interested in the whole business, he wanted to sleep. But the ticket-collector went on: the engineer, who's a very ambitious man, has made up for the delay, and so, madam, the train is no longer behind schedule, and you'll reach your destination exactly on time. The lady thanked him and held out her hand for the ticket, but he felt like talking some more—about the engineer and about the tortoise that Pamfile had found in a park. The woman didn't quite understand whether Pamfile was the name of the engineer or the tortoise, but of course she didn't ask. She thanked him again and caught hold of the ticket, which had been held un-punched in the collector's hand. When she tried to pull it away from him, he looked at her with surprise and let it go—then, a moment later, asked for it again apologetically as he'd forgotten to punch it. He backed out of the compartment, and from the door said something else about the engineer, which made it clear not only that his name wasn't Pamfile, but that he couldn't stand the animal with which the engineer shared certain character traits: particularly, pigheadedness and stupidity.

The Italian wanted to know what the ticket-collector had said, and so the woman was forced to give as coherent an account of it as possible. But since she hadn't understood very well the whole business about the engineer, she left it out of her summary and gave the tortoise a bigger role instead. Delighted with the way she spoke, the *moustachu* didn't seem at all surprised that grown-up men could quarrel over a tortoise introduced by an aging lover of paradoxes. He laughed gustily and pointed to the peasant, or rather to the wicker basket from which the fish's head had appeared for a few moments. The woman laughed too. Both remained cheerful until the train pulled into the next station, where the woman caught sight of a man running along the platform with a bunch of flowers in his hand. A bunch of roses.

THE STREETCAR WAS PACKED: PEOPLE WERE IRRITABLE, PERHAPS with good reason, and in any case ready to pick a fight. A terrible racket. I pushed my way to the front, beside the driver, and asked him as politely as possible to hurry up: "I'll miss the train, you see, I've just received my draft papers. I'm late." He turned and looked at me for a second but said nothing. "There's no point stopping anywhere, the streetcar's too full already." That must have really infuriated him: I saw him turn first red and then yellow. He began to shout: "Get out of here! Who's driving, me or you?" "Okay, but . . ." "You want us to get derailed, is that it?" "You want us to get derailed!" a well-dressed, square-jawed man chimed in. "He's a hoodlum, a dangerous type." What could I do? I shut up. Then I felt someone stroking my hand. A soft, thick hand had placed itself on mine. It gave me courage. "I'll miss my train," I almost shouted, "I've missed so many trains. I have to get to the station, I have to buy some flowers! She likes them so much." "I like flowers too": a voice behind me, no doubt the woman whose breasts were glued to my shoulder blades in the crowded car. Her stomach was bulging like a pillow. "Don't distract the driver!" someone shouted. "Keep quiet! Shut up!" echoed others. "But this man's in a hurry, don't you see?" She had a pleasant voice, like the woman who always answered the telephone at the station, like Maria's, like Magda's. "He can get a taxi if he's in such a hurry!" We were packed in so tight that I couldn't see the woman behind me, but I could feel her warm breasts and belly. I spoke to her, twisting my head around so that my chin rubbed against my shoulder. I couldn't see her. But I had to say something. "I'm in a hurry, madam. My girlfriend's given birth to a fish weighing ten pounds—right now it's in the arms of his grandfather, and the old man is so happy, just so happy. To tell the truth, I would have liked it to be a perch. But what can we do? The decision is out of our hands." The woman squeezed my hand. Taking advantage of a sudden shift in the crowd to my right, and paying no heed to the square-jawed man on whose toes I was treading, I made an effort to turn around and found myself face to face with the young woman. In fact, I was holding her in my arms. She lowered her eyes and said: "I'm expecting too. And I'd like it to be a barbel." "And the father? What does he say?" She didn't answer.

It was the same with Maria. At first she cried, then she confessed everything to me. We were on the shore of a lake: she loved to swim, and she made for the deep, cold water under some willows on the other side. I sat reading on the shore. She had lowered her eyes in the same way.

"You must be a happy man now you've got a son."

"Yes, ten pounds," I repeated.

"Is he your first?"

"Yes. Or rather no, but the other one died a long time ago."

"Was it also . . . ?"

"No, he was a peacock. He was so beautiful, with a little golden beak and some russet streaks in his plumage. But he was too frail."

Was it just me, or had the woman's belly begun to swell? I tried to hold in my own stomach to make some room for her. I saw beads of sweat on her forehead. I felt her squeezing my hand, grasping my fingers. I called out to the driver to stop. "Get out of the way! Move!" People fell back, even though they didn't really understand what was happening, while the man with the square jaw, who was now between me and the driver, also called for the streetcar to stop—which is what it did. No one dared to protest, or even to speak. Silence reigned. And the woman's belly split open, with a whistling sound that then turned into a strange and extraordinarily beautiful music; a bluish light descended on the streetcar, and there came into the world first a barbel, then two white angora rabbits, and a rose. The woman smiled, proud and happy. The man with the square jaw began to applaud, bravo! bravo!, and everyone took up the refrain. It was a stupid kind of glee: everyone rejoiced without knowing why as they jostled to see the little creatures who'd appeared in their midst. In fact, they didn't deserve such honor. The bluish light faded out, but the gaiety in the streetcar became even more loud and vulgar. I thought that only a miracle would let me to catch the train now. And I don't believe in miracles. The woman clasped her offspring to her breast happily: the barbel squeaked gently and the rose stroked its cheek. The rabbits ran through the room.

"You'll be late," M. said. "Get up, come on, get up!" He tried to take her in his arms, but she pulled herself away; then he opened his eyes, jumped out of bed, and began to dress. "Don't forget the flowers! And remember: the elevator's not working." Three floors are nothing, he said to himself, and he ran down the stairs two by two. There was a blinding light outside, from a spotlight. A tank drove down the middle of the road and disappeared into a side street. They were filming something. He took a few steps and stopped in front of the driver's courtyard: most of the lights were aimed at him. One of the women had tripped and fallen on the pig, and now the man was frenziedly sticking the knife into the heap of flesh beneath him, while the other women tried vainly to stay his hand. The child was propped against the wall, playing a flute. The man started walking again. Confused by the light, a dog ran out from behind a fence and bumped straight into him. He only just avoided falling. He broke into a run, although clearly he could no longer catch the bus that was waiting at the stop. After a hundred yards he came to a stop. An old man was sitting beside a suitcase, or rather a kind of army trunk, and looking around him with an air of bewilderment. A few passing cyclists flung some insults or tasteless jokes at him. The old man was inspecting his hands. He looked weary.

He sped off following the route of the bus, but soon he was forced to stop because a group of people were blocking the street. "What's going on?" "A fish. They've found a fish." "It got lost." "It's not a fish: it's a child in the shape of a fish." "It has a head like a fish." "It looks nice, though." "Look how it's moving." "It's not a child, it's a dwarf." "It's a monster. More and more monsters have been appearing recently." "It's horrible." "Look how it's crying, the poor thing!" "The poor monster!" "It's not a monster, it's just ugly." "What frail little legs it has!"

I pushed my way through and set off again: what did I care about all that nonsense? They ought to prohibit people from gathering like that, especially in the streets, on the pavement. I broke into a run, thinking that I would find a taxi. A line of green tanks painted with stars were sliding merrily on their treads. What if I got a tank to take me? I began to make desperate signs with my handkerchief, which, if truth be told, was not exactly clean. Maybe that's why I stopped. In the end I found a taxi, a small purple taxi with a lily on its hood. It also had a pair of wings, for customers in a hurry, except that the device to start them up was broken. I got into the taxi; I hadn't noticed from outside that some people were already in it. A peasant with a basket in his arms was dozing beside the driver. I sat in the seat behind the driver, next to a woman in black who had a string bag full of fish and bread on her lap. It seemed to me that I had seen her before, maybe on a bus or somewhere; there are some faces that stay with you. Beside her, a man with a moustache was smiling wildly and showing his teeth. I turned and began to look out of the window. The streets were no longer so crowded, and the driver was madly racing along. The man with the moustache said something in Italian, to which the woman said something in reply. They spoke the names of some medicines or flowers. But I'm not really sure. The taxi came to a road on which there were mostly trucks and bicycles—workers on their way home from work. Then I suddenly found myself in front of the garden. Ion was standing at the gate and seemed very pleased to see me. I wanted to pay, but the driver refused to accept any money. I felt a little offended. "Do you love her?" he asked me. "I don't know. I don't know anymore."

M. was sitting at the little table with a colored umbrella, in among the flower beds.

"You'll be late if you don't hurry," she said. And he answered with irritation: "Can't you see I'm hurrying? I hurry all the time." M. laughed. He did too. "The bike's in the garage, you know. And don't forget the flowers."

He went into the garage, took the bicycle, put the bunch of flowers in the seat rack, and moved off. Ion opened the gate wide and greeted me by raising the shears to his head. I was in a hurry, of course. Two more cyclists appeared from a courtyard: a man and a woman. He was wearing a sailor's jersey and a top hat. She was dressed in black. I overtook them, turned left, and came to the beltway. I sat up in the seat so that I could pedal faster. I accidentally bumped into an old man, who was carrying a green army trunk on the edge of the sidewalk. I hit him with my shoulder and only just managed to keep my balance. I stopped and turned towards him. The old man crossed to the other side of the street, without even looking left or right: a truck almost ran him over. I was hot. I'd better go back. I'll tell her there were no more tickets left, they'd all been sold, the station was packed with people. If she believes me, fine, if not, it's her business! The old man stopped to wipe the perspiration from his brow. It was terribly hot. How good it would have been to have a straw hat, or a cap, or at least that cyclist's top hat—a top hat or even a white or pink or yellow opera hat.

He returned to the hotel. And, what the hell: M. wasn't in the room; the key was hanging at the reception desk. The elevator girl smiled at him, but he wasn't in the mood for her. The pharmacist and a captain or colonel or whatever were also in the elevator. The girl winked at him, but he looked away. Then she became angry, took out a miniature pistol and fired twice: the pharmacist and the captain fell on their knees, each clutching his heart. The elevator stopped.

"Are we there?" he asked.

"Yes," the girl replied. The gun was still smoking in her hand.

They went into the room. When he kissed her and fumbled to remove her blouse, he realized that he had forgotten her name.

"What did you say your name was?"

"Bravo! You've forgotten it," she reproached him.

"I'm sorry, I just can't remember."

The girl took off the blouse herself and said:

"It begins with M . . ."

"Ah, yes!" he exclaimed, as he pushed her on to the bed.

The whole thing lasted no more than ten minutes. He was in a hurry.

"You know, I ought to be going. I absolutely have to meet someone at the station. No, I can't not go."

He dressed, the girl dressed, and they left. They agreed to meet on the beach, in front of the refreshment stand, then he set off running towards the bus stop. He got on at the last moment. As I stepped on to the bus I felt an urge to look back, as if someone had called out or tapped me on the shoulder or perhaps just looked at me, in the way you look at a person who seems familiar and whose name you want to call out. What name? I didn't turn around, I climbed the last step and asked for a ticket, then occupied the seat behind the driver. The pharmacist and the mustachioed captain were sitting on the next seat over. I pretended not to see them: I didn't feel like talking, I was in a hurry. After the bus collided with a tank, I went off to catch a streetcar. There I came across someone else I knew, as well as a woman who looked like M. Then I realized that the streetcar was going in the wrong direction. What did I want, in fact? To get to the station. Well, the streetcar wasn't going to the station, but towards the sea. The ticket-seller chuckled with delight at the fix I'd got myself in. I too started laughing. Everyone was heading for the beach. "It's hot," she bellowed, as if I was deaf. In fact, I wasn't speaking only for myself but for the whole car. All the passengers applauded and shouted bravo. The ticket-seller pointed at me: "You see, he's laughing himself. He no longer has anything to lose." More applause. I bent over and continued to laugh, even exaggerating a little to please the other passengers—that is, the audience. He's laughing, he's happy. The ticket-seller opened her blouse and began to remove her skirt. The others undressed too. I went on laughing, even though no one was applauding any longer.

The streetcar reached the beach and stopped. We got off, in an excellent mood. M. was waiting for me with a large bunch of roses. We hugged each other for a long time.

"Come on, hurry up!" He took her in his arms, but she managed to tear herself away. "You'll be late if you don't get going." He pulled the duvet over him and she began to tickle his heels. He couldn't stand that. He jumped up and looked for his clothes to get dressed; the white coffee had gone cold, so he gulped it straight down. "Don't forget the flowers!" He took the briefcase under his arm and went on to the veranda. As he descended the steps into the garden, he noticed a shaven-headed man in homespun clothes leaning against the wall of the house. They looked at each other for a moment, then the boy started running towards the gate.

"So, to get from M_1 to M_2 . . ."

"M what?"

"There you go again! M for goddamn monkeys. I told you it doesn't matter."

"Right, go on."

"So, to get from M_1 to M_2, whether you like it or not you have to pass through a point halfway between the two. Here, okay? But to get there you have to pass through this other point, which is also a halfway point, understand? And to get to that you have to pass through this other point, which is also half the distance."

The ticket-collector divided the line on the sheet of paper into smaller and smaller segments.

"There'll always be a point through which you have to pass."

"And what if I jump, or if I pass through at high speed?"

"Look, let's try it a different way: something more concrete. Let's say you catch a bus, okay? You get on the bus somewhere near home, to go to the station."

"Right, I've got you."

"Good. Now, doesn't that distance also have a halfway point, a point dividing it in two?"

"Of course it does."

"And to reach that point, don't you have to pass through another point that's half of that half? And further on—I mean: before then, yes, before then—to get to that point don't you first have to pass through another point that is also a halfway point? And so on . . ."

"I don't understand," the engineer admitted, scratching his hairy chest.

The ticket-collector took a deep breath and drew two parallel lines on the paper—or rather, lines that he meant to be parallel, but that's not important.

"Look, this is a streetcar route. Let's say you get on at one end to get to the other end."

With furrowed brows, the engineer leaned over the sheet of paper that the other man was holding in his hand.

"How are we doing?" the ticket-collector asked.

"Fine, that's clear enough."

"Well, this line has a number of points along it: that is, tram stops. Okay?"

"Okay."

"But the distance from one stop to another can itself be subdivided by a further series of points, this time closer to each another. And those shorter distances can, in turn, be split into even shorter distances."

The engineer was shaking from the effort of concentration. Now he had to understand. Yet the ticket-collector's voice was more and more hesitant.

"Any distance, however short, can always be divided further."

He stopped. He was on the wrong track. The streetcar had been a stupid example: it was going nowhere.

"I'm sorry," the ticket-collector said, "I made a mistake. I got a bit lost."

The engineer relaxed and said with a kindly smile, "Well, it's certainly interesting. Yes, interesting, but hard to demonstrate like that, just with a pencil and paper."

"It can be done even without a pencil," the ticket-collector said with irritation. "It's a question of logic."

"Ah, logic," the other man said, looking at his watch and nodding. "Why the hell don't they let us get moving? We've been stuck here a quarter of an hour."

The ticket-collector's eyes flashed. He raised the pencil like a conductor's baton.

"Let's say a child sets off from home to go to school. He needs to cover a distance n by bus or streetcar, on a bicycle or on foot. Well, first he has to cover the distance between home and the bus stop: he must therefore go to the end of his street, turn left, cross the street, then another street, and go onto the boulevard where the bus runs. But to reach the end of the street, he first has to pass in front of all the houses on one side or the other. Do you understand? And, before that, he has to leave home by the gate, that is, to pass through the garden, and in order to reach the garden he must go down the veranda steps onto the gravel path. There are so many distances to cover, so many movements to make."

The ticket-collector came to a stop, wrapped up in his thoughts. The engineer gaped at him, quite simply, then coughed and tried to mutter something; he spoke a word or just a few sounds, raised his arm and let it fall again: he didn't understand anything at all.

The stationmaster still hadn't given the signal for them to leave. The ticket-collector looked out of the window: the platform was deserted.

HE TOOK OFF HIS SHIRT AND LOOKED AT HIMSELF FOR A MOMENT in the mirror, wearing only a T-shirt on top, then donned his driver's cap and went into the yard. The boy sat cross-legged, against the wall of the house next door, playing a flute or whistle or whatever it was. In the street, he saw a shaven-headed old man dragging along an army trunk. He stopped to wipe his brow and neck with a handkerchief. It was hot. No longer listening to the other men, he sat motionless on the edge of the bed, his eyes focused on the iron-plate door full of scratches: rivers, forests, railway lines, gardens, wonderful rose gardens, and Ion with those huge shears from which he was never parted. A chicken darted out from behind a bush. She looked around, a little frightened, then started walking along the path; she stopped from time to time to look for little insects in the gravel. He moved away from the window and sat down on the wooden floor. The train was ready to leave, he had only to press a button, then another one to switch the points so that it wouldn't hit the other train rattling along in the opposite direction. The woman was sewing, her head bent slightly forward and to one side—as in the painting on the wall, except that there, instead of working on a jacket, she was holding in her arms a chubby pink infant.

The driver turned his eyes to the pigsty at the back of the yard—or, rather, to the heap of boards where the pigs were kept. He smiled. The boy's flute filled the whole space with music.

"Why do you keep gawking at the door like that?" a voice asked angrily, from one of the beds at the back. Someone had used a nail to scratch a straight line between the lock and the peephole, then divided the line into a number of equal segments, as if to demonstrate a geometrical proof. Or perhaps he'd only meant to suggest a railway line, and who knows how long he stared at the wretched mark on which his imagination had placed a long train with many cars and two engines. He pressed another button: the signal wasn't working, of course, so he made do with changing tracks again. A fish was passing, in flight above the garden.

He walked resolutely towards the pigsty, but stopped halfway, rubbed his beard, and turned round to look at the façade of the house. He called out a woman's name: Maria or Mariana, and one of the windows opened to reveal a head with long blond hair. The driver shouted for the woman to come down. The head moved in a gesture of agreement. "Come down, I need you all down here," he added. Then he called another, longer name: probably Magdalena, or Marilena. His voice was hoarse, and he was barely articulating the words. He again rubbed his beard and pulled the cap over his ears. The woman looked at the boy, who continued to play with the train. An indulgent smile was playing on her lips: he'll grow up, she said to herself. Then she thought of the other, if that's the right way of putting it. A large rust stain was visible above the peephole. A swamp. A swamp teeming with snakes, frogs, and rats.

The driver reappeared with a huge knife, took a few steps towards the pigsty, and stopped. He bent down to place the knife on one of the slabs in the yard, then stood up straight and remained still. The flute gave out a dribble of short clear sounds: a simple, repetitive melody. After a certain point, although the player kept the instrument in his mouth, nothing more could be heard. It was quiet. Only the steps of someone running in the street. A man holding a bunch of flowers dashed in front of the gate. The driver shouted Mariana or Magdalena again, but this time the window didn't open. He shrugged his shoulders and headed towards the sty. He stopped to listen in front of the door: not a sound. He touched the marks above the peephole with his fingertips, even trying to look out through the opening. But of course he could see nothing: it was shut on the outside.

The driver opened the little door and stood to one side. Moments later, the pig came out fearlessly—even displaying a kind of dignity charged with meaning. The driver wasn't interested in such matters: he turned on his heels and again yelled for the women to come. Finally the three of them were advancing slowly, tall and good-looking, in long pink-and-white silk dresses, each carrying a large white bowl. The man drove the pig to the middle of the yard, not meeting the slightest resistance. Its placid eyes were staring towards the closed door. The others were talking, arguing, making fun of poor Milescu. From time to time they turned their attention to him, came and surrounded him, plied him with good-natured questions. And he had to answer: they were natural questions, asked with kindness, not only curiosity, about his family, his children. He pushed another button and both trains came to a halt. The woman nervously raised her eyes. A screeching could be heard on the tracks.

The boy still had the flute in his mouth, but no sound was coming from it. In the street, a man passed with a wooden, green-painted suitcase, then a young man who seemed in a great hurry. And a cyclist. Next, a child running with a briefcase under one arm and a bunch of flowers under the other. Nothing more. A tank passed a little later.

The pig was waiting calmly. The man filled his lungs with air and, mechanically stroking the peak of his cap, issued a brief order. Powerful hands seized him and laid him out on an iron table. He thought he could hear two knives being rubbed together. He closed his eyes. The child was again sitting on the wooden floor, in front of the electric trains that clanked melodiously on tracks coiled in two or three figure eights. The woman was sewing a button on a jacket. When he came round, he again saw the door and the scratch mark running like a railway from the lock to the peephole: a straight line in equal segments.

The sun had risen above their heads. The knife was gleaming beside one of the pig's feet. Next to the wall, the waiting women held large white bowls in their arms. With a sudden, powerful movement, the driver pushed the pig on its back and picked up the knife. The women solemnly drew closer. The man's arm struck eagerly. The knife cut deep into the pig's belly; it gave out no more than two or three grunts. The driver looked for a moment at the dripping knife and struck again. And again. The blood spurted like a jet from an artesian well. The women approached with the bowls. Their dresses became soiled with blood.

The man's T-shirt was now red. One of the women stumbled and toppled over the animal's body onto her back.

For a remote observer—for example, that young man hurrying along with his comically big steps, holding a bunch of flowers so awkwardly that you'd think he was carrying a chicken from the market, a little frightened and disgusted—for such an observer, who stops to gawk with curiosity at what is, in the end, just a banal, everyday scene, it looks as though the driver continues to strike blindly with his dripping knife, driving it into the heap of flesh and blood-smeared garments, while the other women run away or throw down their bowls and try to stay the man's pitiless hand, one of them falling on her knees, another raising her arms to heaven in a gesture of prayer, and then the flute is heard once more, a soft sweet melody spreads far into the distance, heard even by Ion as he putters among the rose beds, and by the woman sewing buttons on the homespun jacket and occasionally casting a fond look at the little boy on the wooden floor in front of his trains—a simple melody that finds its way up to and through that door that's scratched in all kinds of ways, and I sit on the edge of the bed, my hands resting submissively on my knees, and listen to the sounds of the flute that continue without interruption, the same melody played over and over again *da capo*, with such conviction that the driver's raised arm freezes and the women too remain still, while little drops of blood, in time with the flute, drip down from the knife blade. The sky is blue and glowing.

PETROS ABATZOGLOU, *What Does Mrs. Freeman Want?*
PIERRE ALBERT-BIROT, *Grabinoulor.*
YUZ ALESHKOVSKY, *Kangaroo.*
FELIPE ALFAU, *Chromos.*
Locos.
IVAN ÂNGELO, *The Celebration.*
The Tower of Glass.
DAVID ANTIN, *Talking.*
DJUNA BARNES, *Ladies Almanack.*
Ryder.
JOHN BARTH, *LETTERS.*
Sabbatical.
DONALD BARTHELME, *The King.*
Paradise.
SVETISLAV BASARA, *Chinese Letter.*
MARK BINELLI, *Sacco and Vanzetti Must Die!*
ANDREI BITOV, *Pushkin House.*
LOUIS PAUL BOON, *Chapel Road.*
Summer in Termuren.
ROGER BOYLAN, *Killoyle.*
IGNÁCIO DE LOYOLA BRANDÃO, *Teeth under the Sun.*
Zero.
CHRISTINE BROOKE-ROSE, *Amalgamemnon.*
BRIGID BROPHY, *In Transit.*
MEREDITH BROSNAN, *Mr. Dynamite.*
GERALD L. BRUNS,
Modern Poetry and the Idea of Language.
GABRIELLE BURTON, *Heartbreak Hotel.*
MICHEL BUTOR, *Degrees.*
Mobile.
Portrait of the Artist as a Young Ape.
G. CABRERA INFANTE, *Infante's Inferno.*
Three Trapped Tigers.
JULIETA CAMPOS, *The Fear of Losing Eurydice.*
ANNE CARSON, *Eros the Bittersweet.*
CAMILO JOSÉ CELA, *The Family of Pascual Duarte.*
The Hive.
LOUIS-FERDINAND CÉLINE, *Castle to Castle.*
Conversations with Professor Y.
London Bridge.
North.
Rigadoon.
HUGO CHARTERIS, *The Tide Is Right.*
JEROME CHARYN, *The Tar Baby.*
MARC CHOLODENKO, *Mordechai Schamz.*
EMILY HOLMES COLEMAN, *The Shutter of Snow.*
ROBERT COOVER, *A Night at the Movies.*
STANLEY CRAWFORD, *Some Instructions to My Wife.*
ROBERT CREELEY, *Collected Prose.*
RENÉ CREVEL, *Putting My Foot in It.*
RALPH CUSACK, *Cadenza.*
SUSAN DAITCH, *L.C.*
Storytown.
NIGEL DENNIS, *Cards of Identity.*
PETER DIMOCK,
A Short Rhetoric for Leaving the Family.
ARIEL DORFMAN, *Konfidenz.*
COLEMAN DOWELL, *The Houses of Children.*
Island People.
Too Much Flesh and Jabez.
RIKKI DUCORNET, *The Complete Butcher's Tales.*
The Fountains of Neptune.
The Jade Cabinet.
Phosphor in Dreamland.
The Stain.
The Word "Desire."
WILLIAM EASTLAKE, *The Bamboo Bed.*
Castle Keep.
Lyric of the Circle Heart.
JEAN ECHENOZ, *Chopin's Move.*
STANLEY ELKIN, *A Bad Man.*
Boswell: A Modern Comedy.
Criers and Kibitzers, Kibitzers and Criers.
The Dick Gibson Show.
The Franchiser.
George Mills.
The Living End.
The MacGuffin.
The Magic Kingdom.
Mrs. Ted Bliss.

The Rabbi of Lud.
Van Gogh's Room at Arles.
ANNIE ERNAUX, *Cleaned Out.*
LAUREN FAIRBANKS, *Muzzle Thyself.*
Sister Carrie.
LESLIE A. FIEDLER,
Love and Death in the American Novel.
GUSTAVE FLAUBERT, *Bouvard and Pécuchet.*
FORD MADOX FORD, *The March of Literature.*
JON FOSSE, *Melancholy.*
MAX FRISCH, *I'm Not Stiller.*
CARLOS FUENTES, *Christopher Unborn.*
Distant Relations.
Terra Nostra.
Where the Air Is Clear.
JANICE GALLOWAY, *Foreign Parts.*
The Trick Is to Keep Breathing.
WILLIAM H. GASS, *The Tunnel.*
Willie Masters' Lonesome Wife.
ETIENNE GILSON, *The Arts of the Beautiful.*
Forms and Substances in the Arts.
C. S. GISCOMBE, *Giscome Road.*
Here.
DOUGLAS GLOVER, *Bad News of the Heart.*
The Enamoured Knight.
KAREN ELIZABETH GORDON, *The Red Shoes.*
GEORGI GOSPODINOV, *Natural Novel.*
JUAN GOYTISOLO, *Marks of Identity.*
PATRICK GRAINVILLE, *The Cave of Heaven.*
HENRY GREEN, *Blindness.*
Concluding.
Doting.
Nothing.
JIŘÍ GRUŠA, *The Questionnaire.*
JOHN HAWKES, *Whistlejacket.*
AIDAN HIGGINS, *A Bestiary.*
Bornholm Night-Ferry.
Flotsam and Jetsam.
Langrishe, Go Down.
Scenes from a Receding Past.
Windy Arbours.
ALDOUS HUXLEY, *Antic Hay.*
Crome Yellow.
Point Counter Point.
Those Barren Leaves.
Time Must Have a Stop.
MIKHAIL IOSSEL AND JEFF PARKER, EDS., *Amerika: Contemporary Russians View the United States.*
GERT JONKE, *Geometric Regional Novel.*
JACQUES JOUET, *Mountain R.*
HUGH KENNER, *The Counterfeiters.*
Flaubert, Joyce and Beckett: The Stoic Comedians.
Joyce's Voices.
DANILO KIŠ, *Garden, Ashes.*
A Tomb for Boris Davidovich.
ANITA KONKKA, *A Fool's Paradise.*
TADEUSZ KONWICKI, *A Minor Apocalypse.*
The Polish Complex.
MENIS KOUMANDAREAS, *Koula.*
ELAINE KRAF, *The Princess of 72nd Street.*
JIM KRUSOE, *Iceland.*
EWA KURYLUK, *Century 21.*
VIOLETTE LEDUC, *La Bâtarde.*
DEBORAH LEVY, *Billy and Girl.*
Pillow Talk in Europe and Other Places.
JOSÉ LEZAMA LIMA, *Paradiso.*
ROSA LIKSOM, *Dark Paradise.*
OSMAN LINS, *Avalovara.*
The Queen of the Prisons of Greece.
ALF MAC LOCHLAINN, *The Corpus in the Library.*
Out of Focus.
RON LOEWINSOHN, *Magnetic Field(s).*
D. KEITH MANO, *Take Five.*
BEN MARCUS, *The Age of Wire and String.*
WALLACE MARKFIELD, *Teitlebaum's Window.*
To an Early Grave.
DAVID MARKSON, *Reader's Block.*
Springer's Progress.
Wittgenstein's Mistress.

SELECTED DALKEY ARCHIVE PAPERBACKS

CAROLE MASO, *AVA.*
LADISLAV MATEJKA AND KRYSTYNA POMORSKA, EDS.,
  *Readings in Russian Poetics: Formalist and
  Structuralist Views.*
HARRY MATHEWS,
  *The Case of the Persevering Maltese: Collected
  Essays.*
  Cigarettes.
  The Conversions.
  The Human Country: New and Collected Stories.
  The Journalist.
  My Life in CIA.
  Singular Pleasures.
  The Sinking of the Odradek Stadium.
  Tlooth.
  20 Lines a Day.
ROBERT L. MCLAUGHLIN, ED.,
  *Innovations: An Anthology of Modern &
  Contemporary Fiction.*
HERMAN MELVILLE, *The Confidence-Man.*
STEVEN MILLHAUSER, *The Barnum Museum.*
  In the Penny Arcade.
RALPH J. MILLS, JR., *Essays on Poetry.*
OLIVE MOORE, *Spleen.*
NICHOLAS MOSLEY, *Accident.*
  Assassins.
  Catastrophe Practice.
  Children of Darkness and Light.
  Experience and Religion.
  The Hesperides Tree.
  Hopeful Monsters.
  Imago Bird.
  Impossible Object.
  Inventing God.
  Judith.
  Look at the Dark.
  Natalie Natalia.
  Serpent.
  Time at War.
  The Uses of Slime Mould: Essays of Four Decades.
WARREN F. MOTTE, JR.,
  Fables of the Novel: French Fiction since 1990.
  Oulipo: A Primer of Potential Literature.
YVES NAVARRE, *Our Share of Time.*
  Sweet Tooth.
DOROTHY NELSON, *In Night's City.*
  Tar and Feathers.
WILFRIDO D. NOLLEDO, *But for the Lovers.*
FLANN O'BRIEN, *At Swim-Two-Birds.*
  At War.
  The Best of Myles.
  The Dalkey Archive.
  Further Cuttings.
  The Hard Life.
  The Poor Mouth.
  The Third Policeman.
CLAUDE OLLIER, *The Mise-en-Scène.*
PATRIK OUŘEDNÍK, *Europeana.*
FERNANDO DEL PASO, *Palinuro of Mexico.*
ROBERT PINGET, *The Inquisitory.*
  Mahu or The Material.
  Trio.
RAYMOND QUENEAU, *The Last Days.*
  Odile.
  Pierrot Mon Ami.
  Saint Glinglin.
ANN QUIN, *Berg.*
  Passages.
  Three.
  Tripticks.
ISHMAEL REED, *The Free-Lance Pallbearers.*
  The Last Days of Louisiana Red.
  Reckless Eyeballing.
  The Terrible Threes.
  The Terrible Twos.
  Yellow Back Radio Broke-Down.
JULIÁN RÍOS, *Larva: A Midsummer Night's Babel.*
  Poundemonium.
AUGUSTO ROA BASTOS, *I the Supreme.*
JACQUES ROUBAUD, *The Great Fire of London.*
  Hortense in Exile.

Hortense Is Abducted.
  The Plurality of Worlds of Lewis.
  The Princess Hoppy.
  *The Form of a City Changes Faster, Alas,
  Than the Human Heart.*
  Some Thing Black.
LEON S. ROUDIEZ, *French Fiction Revisited.*
VEDRANA RUDAN, *Night.*
LYDIE SALVAYRE, *The Company of Ghosts.*
  Everyday Life.
  The Lecture.
LUIS RAFAEL SÁNCHEZ, *Macho Camacho's Beat.*
SEVERO SARDUY, *Cobra & Maitreya.*
NATHALIE SARRAUTE, *Do You Hear Them?*
  Martereau.
  The Planetarium.
ARNO SCHMIDT, *Collected Stories.*
  Nobodaddy's Children.
CHRISTINE SCHUTT, *Nightwork.*
GAIL SCOTT, *My Paris.*
JUNE AKERS SEESE,
  Is This What Other Women Feel Too?
  What Waiting Really Means.
AURELIE SHEEHAN, *Jack Kerouac Is Pregnant.*
VIKTOR SHKLOVSKY, *Knight's Move.*
  A Sentimental Journey: Memoirs 1917-1922.
  Theory of Prose.
  Third Factory.
  Zoo, or Letters Not about Love.
JOSEF ŠKVORECKÝ,
  The Engineer of Human Souls.
CLAUDE SIMON, *The Invitation.*
GILBERT SORRENTINO, *Aberration of Starlight.*
  Blue Pastoral.
  Crystal Vision.
  Imaginative Qualities of Actual Things.
  Mulligan Stew.
  Pack of Lies.
  Red the Fiend.
  The Sky Changes.
  Something Said.
  Splendide-Hôtel.
  Steelwork.
  Under the Shadow.
W. M. SPACKMAN, *The Complete Fiction.*
GERTRUDE STEIN, *Lucy Church Amiably.*
  The Making of Americans.
  A Novel of Thank You.
PIOTR SZEWC, *Annihilation.*
STEFAN THEMERSON, *Hobson's Island.*
  The Mystery of the Sardine.
  Tom Harris.
JEAN-PHILIPPE TOUSSAINT, *Television.*
DUMITRU TSEPENEAG, *Vain Art of the Fugue.*
ESTHER TUSQUETS, *Stranded.*
DUBRAVKA UGRESIC, *Lend Me Your Character.*
  Thank You for Not Reading.
MATI UNT, *Things in the Night.*
ELOY URROZ, *The Obstacles.*
LUISA VALENZUELA, *He Who Searches.*
BORIS VIAN, *Heartsnatcher.*
PAUL WEST, *Words for a Deaf Daughter & Gala.*
CURTIS WHITE, *America's Magic Mountain.*
  The Idea of Home.
  Memories of My Father Watching TV.
  *Monstrous Possibility: An Invitation to
  Literary Politics.*
  Requiem.
DIANE WILLIAMS, *Excitability: Selected Stories.*
  Romancer Erector.
DOUGLAS WOOLF, *Wall to Wall.*
  Ya! & John-Juan.
PHILIP WYLIE, *Generation of Vipers.*
MARGUERITE YOUNG, *Angel in the Forest.*
  Miss MacIntosh, My Darling.
REYOUNG, *Unbabbling.*
ZORAN ŽIVKOVIĆ, *Hidden Camera.*
LOUIS ZUKOFSKY, *Collected Fiction.*
SCOTT ZWIREN, *God Head.*